Praise for B

THE SUM

MW00682088

"...Draga likes to mess with traditional stuff like Orcs and wizards and black conspiracies, but he has just enough creativity to make it his own."

- Caleb Hill, Acerbic Writing

"3 out of 4 stars...a light read for anyone who loves fantasy and can't get enough of it."

- Norma Rudolph, Online Book Club

"...Draga does a stellar job of mixing likeable characters with shady scoundrels that become unlikely heroes... I cannot wait for the second book."

- Stephen Fisher, Readers' Favorite

THE SUMMERLARK ELF

THE FOUR KINGDOMS SAGA: BOOK ONE

BY
BRANDON DRAGA

This book is a work of fiction. All characters in this novel are fictitious. Any resemblance to actual events or locales or persons, living or dead, is entirely coincidental.

The Summerlark Elf
Copyright © 2015 by Brandon Draga

Cover Art, Interior Art, and Map by Deanna Laver

A RPG Book
Published by Realmwalker Publishing Group, Inc.
13290 W. Mill Road
Malcolm, NE 68402

www.realmwalkerpublishing.com

ISBN 978-1-943670-10-9
First Edition: 2013
Second Edition: 2015

Printed in the United States of America

The Four Kingdoms Saga

Book One: The Summerlark Elf

Book Two: The Missing Thane's War

Acknowledgments

When I first set out to write this book it felt, in many ways, like the most self-centered thing I'd ever worked on. The reality of the matter is that nothing could be further from the truth. Yes, the words and how they fit together are all mine, but this was far from a solo endeavor, and I want to take a moment to take note of everyone who was so integral in this process.

To everyone who took the time to read my initial drafts, your kind compliments tempered by your honest critiques helped me hone this book into what it had the potential to be from its onset.

To my gaming group, Nick, Matthew, Andrea, and Deanna, your time spent being subjected to my fiendish designs unknowingly helped me sharpen my storytelling immeasurably.

To my family, Mom and Dad, Ryan, Elliott, and Nikki, you all have been nothing if not supportive and encouraging, and more than willing to deal with my hours upon hours spent glued to a keyboard and sequestered from the real world. An added special thanks to Nikki, who was very much a cornerstone in the foundations of getting this story started.

Finally, to Deanna, who has been a muse, a confidant, and the true matriarch of the Overhill family. You will always be my favourite halfling.

N

E

W

S

Maladrin

Ivyd River

The Windswept Sea

Barkaan

Ghest

E. Fellowdale

W. Fellowdale

Khalen Ridge

Delverbrook

Deltharden

Morabendar

Hallowspire

The River Birchmeer

Rheth

The Orharric Mts.

The Dwarven Thaneship

Arvadem

Lohvast

Frostpoint

Heavenguard

Albsryn

Otharkind

The Lohvastine Mts.

PROLOGUE

"**B**loody Hells, Randis, who is that?!" Tessa Summerlark had seen her husband drag in his fair share of oddities and curios in his years as a merchant, some occasionally living things, but never in all her years married to the man had he walked into their home carrying a person.

"Calm yerself, Tess, it ain't what it looks like."

"Oh? My husband walking into my kitchen carrying a pregnant woman in his arms? Please, Randis, explain to me what part of this I'm misinterpreting." The person in Randis Summerlark's arms was, indeed, a woman, swaddled in a cloak and blankets, and very visibly pregnant. Tessa was not throwing about wild accusations at her husband, but that is not to say that certain hypotheses regarding the present situation were not currently playing out in her mind.

Randis paid little mind to his wife's tone, understanding her shock, but also being more aware than she of the urgency of the matter. "Come now, just clear the table. This woman needs help." As Tessa did so, Randis lay the woman gently down. "I found her not five miles outside town. It were like lightning struck the ground just 'afore I came upon her, but different; like there were no clap o' thunder, nor any bolt falling from the sky. Just a flash on the ground and a sound like a great sigh." Randis unfolded the blanket he had wrapped the woman in and unclasped her cloak, revealing two things that left Tessa in a moment of shock: the large gash across the top of the woman's chest, and a thin, youthful face with long, pointed ears.

Tessa covered her mouth, awestruck. "Randis..." she half-whispered "An elf? A fae-folk, here? What're we going to do? If the King's Guard were to find out..."

"They'll not find out." Randis answered as he rummaged through the kitchen cupboards "We've three weeks yet 'afore they come collecting for the year. That gives us time to stitch the lass up, keep her hidden while she gains her strength back, an' send her on her way."

Tessa was going to protest further, but she stopped herself, feeling a hand reach up and clasp hers. Looking down, she saw the elf moving her lips. Instinctively, Tessa bent down to try and listen, hearing the woman whisper to her in soft, if broken Common speech. "Please... too late...I go forth...child..." The woman's whispers gave way to subtle, pained moans as she took her hand from Tessa's and placed it onto her protruding belly.

Randis, hearing the moans, looked over at the table, and immediately ran to fetch a basin of water and some linens. While the Summerlarks had no children, living on a farmstead made them no strangers to birth via livestock. What's more, what Randis lacked in formal education, he made up for in time spent on the road, and in his days as a merchant he had come across far more bizarre happenings than childbirth. As Randis returned to the kitchen, he saw the elf woman was in full-blown labour, a labour he knew she would not survive, and that he feared the child might.

Several hours after the moon had reached its apex in the night sky, Randis knelt at the foot of a shallow, impromptu grave in a small clearing of a wooded area along the perimeter of the farmstead. As he knelt he mumbled a prayer to Lythwin, the only Fae god he knew of. Upon completing his makeshift funeral rite, Randis walked with heavy, burdened feet back to his home, wherein upon entering, he saw his wife sitting, cradling a newborn girl. The child was smaller and more slender than a human child, though not entirely decipherable, save the large, pointed ears that belied her fae heritage. Tessa's look was somber, and evidently more full of questions than answers. She looked at her husband, her eyes on the brink of tears, "What do we do?"

"We keep her." He responded flatly, almost matter-of-factly. "Raise her a Summerlark, and give her a life here." He saw the love in his wife's eyes the minute she looked upon the child, and knew she wouldn't contest that point. He was, however, skirting the obvious.

"And how do we keep them from finding out?" Tessa asked.

"You've lived in this kingdom as long as I, and you know what they'll do..." her voice began to quiver and trail off as her mind filled in the blanks.

Randis sighed heavily, knowing that there was no easy solution, and after several long moments of contemplation, decided upon what he believed in his heart to be the least difficult. Breathing deep, he drew his dagger from the sheath on his belt, and walked toward the child.

CHAPTER ONE

The town of Delverbrook, in the kingdom of Ghest, was not especially large, not in the way that cities such as Forgevale to the north or the Fellowdales to the east were large. It was not so small, however, that it was without its share of less-than-favourable areas. It was in one of these areas that there sat a seedy tavern known as the Oaken Cask. The Cask was not an unclean establishment in the physical sense. In fact the Cask's owner and lead barkeep, an older Elven woman, ensured quite the opposite. The main area of the tavern was fairly well lit, with polished wood tables and a smooth granite bar. Food and drink were reasonably priced, albeit far from gourmet, and one could find board in the rooms above for a fair price as well. There was little, if anything, about the Cask's outward appearance that would suggest that it even belonged in the area of Delverbrook in which it was situated. What made for the Cask's sullen, if ill-discussed reputation, were the Back Rooms.

The Back Rooms were where many of the Cask's patrons conducted business, with the Common currency being less often gold, but flesh, either living or dead, depending on the type of business. It was in one of the Back Rooms that there sat two individuals. One, a half-elf, sat relaxed, idly tuning his mandolin. Beside him sat a halfling, fidgeting uncomfortably in his chair as his feet dangled from it, trying his best to conceal his evidently frayed nerves.

"I don't like this, Erasmus." The halfling stated with a practiced calm "We helped him with that last job, and he told us he wouldn't be contacting us no more." He wrung his hands reflexively for a moment as his cohort continued the nonchalant maintenance of the mandolin. "For Shendré's sake, we're not even members of his guild, though who'd want to be?"

The half-elf gave his instrument a muted strum and, satisfied with its sound, placed it next to him. "O'doc, old friend, be calm." Erasmus spoke with a voice like an aged whiskey; slightly coarse and smoky, but with an underlying smoothness that caused a person to instinctively relax, oftentimes too much if one was not careful. "We've got nothing to fear from Ravenclaw. This'll likely be just another fetch job in some out-of-the-way farming town where the Rats aren't present. Besides, you remember as well as I how well that last job paid."

O'doc couldn't help but admit that his partner was right; to his knowledge, neither he nor Erasmus had ever crossed the River Rats. If they had, one or both of them would have felt the repercussions long before now. The money, too, was quite the draw. The last time the pair helped Ravenclaw secure some mysterious cargo from a band of bugbears who had ransacked a Rats caravan north of Delverbrook, and the payout was handsome enough to allow the two of them to live comfortably for just over two months. Still, though, O'doc couldn't help but feel uneasy as he sat waiting. So on edge was the poor halfling that it took what was left of his control to not leap from his seat as the door opposite where the pair was seated opened with a loud baritone creak.

The object of O'doc's unease, a fellow halfling, strode through the opened door. This halfling was dressed in dingy, tattered clothing. On the streets, no one would think him more than a Common beggar, although the thick gold chain beneath his hole-riddled shirt and the two hearty men flanking his sides belied both his wealth and prominence. He strode to the table with an odd hunched gait, his eyes darting suspiciously as he made his way. Upon hopping onto the chair opposite O'doc and Erasmus, the halfling focused his beady eyes on the pair. "Gentlemen," he began with a crooked yellow grin, "it's been far too long."

"Lannister Ravenclaw," Erasmus subtly bowed, still seated, "to what do we owe the privilege of a requested audience?"

"Oh, come now, bard; you've no need to try and butter my biscuit with formality. After all," Lannister turned his beady gaze to O'doc, "we're all friends here."

O'doc resisted the urge to shudder. So often, he was the mouthpiece of the operation he and Erasmus had concocted for themselves, and yet any time the pair dealt with the River Rats, and especially with Lannister Ravenclaw, he could not help but be filled with this sick unease, the kind a child feels the first time they see blood. In spite of this, however, the halfling retained his composure. "So what's the job?" he asked, trying to mask his distaste with a feigned casual smirk.

Lannister straightened. "Oh? You're talking, O'doc, splendid! Here I thought I'd gone and frightened the poor lamb stiff..." Lannister, who had yet to sit down, walked around the table as he continued. "'S funny, really, I'd always pegged you as the brains and the bard as the looks. Reminds me of something my father told me: he said 'boy, the quickest way for a man to lose his head is to keep his mouth open and let everything inside fall out'..." as he reached the end of the table where the two partners sat, he leaned in close to O'doc, massaging the now petrified halfling's head with one hand. "So let's be a good lamb and make sure that little head stays right where it is, eh?" The whisper was barely audible, but the cold implications it carried were enough to suck all the colour from O'doc's face.

"Ha HA!" Lannister jumped back, clapping his hands together, scurrying to the opposite side of the table and taking a seat. "But the lad is to the point, and the point is this, gentlemen: I've got someone I need you to retrieve."

"Someone? Not exactly our specialty." Erasmus responded, raising an eyebrow "We've done our fair share of jobs for you, but this? We're not bounty hunters."

"It's not a bounty I'm after."

"Kidnappers, then, whatever professional term you want to use. The point is, O'doc and I move two kinds of goods: information, and objects."

"And that," Lannister said, tapping his finger into the table to emphasize the point "is why I called on you. You and your lamb are the best two smugglers and spies-for-hire I know. I need someone found and retrieved, with as little muss or fuss as is possible. Still smuggling, you see, just that you two'll be smuggling living cargo." He turned to face O'doc "What say you, Lambkins?" After a moment of silence, Lannister cocked his head mock-piteously, "Oh, come now, I was just teasing before. You'd do best to share your thoughts with the bard, you are the brains of the outfit, after all."

O'doc began to weigh everything he'd heard up to this point in his head. On the one hand, the River Rats were the most profitable benefactors the pair had worked for, and they certainly could use the money. On the other hand, there was something about the job that didn't sit well with O'doc; the Rats had agents throughout the better parts of the Four Kingdoms, and the fact that Lannister was approaching outside help for this job meant that he needed the pair to go somewhere the Rats could not. Realizing this, the halfling fought through his unease, and opted for a bold tactic. "What's the job going to pay?" he asked flatly.

"Six hundred crowns," Lannister stated with his yellowed grin "half up front, the remainder held until the job is completed." The offer was more than double what Lannister had paid the pair for their last job. This alone was enough to make Erasmus nearly leap from his seat and take the job, but O'doc discreetly motioned him to hold.

"Look Lannister," O'doc now stood, and began to pace with a perceived calm. "It's safe to say that you and your guild have a fair bit of coin stashed up, am I right?" The halfling didn't expect an answer, but all the same he turned and stared straight at Lannister, albeit largely to try and avoid the sight of his bodyguards. "Now, I don't know who's lining your pocket for this job, but if you expect us to sneak in and out of Hallowspire undetected..." he paused, noticing the subtle change in Lannister's expression to that of genuine surprise. "I think it's safe to say you could offer my partner and me something a bit more fair. Say, three hundred pieces up front..." a tiny smirk began to form at one side of O'doc's mouth "and seven hundred more upon return?"

There was a moment of painful, lingering tension. The two halflings stared at one another for what seemed like an eternity. O'doc took a huge risk, but a calculated one; the money Lannister had offered the pair meant that the job would be in a city, and the only city where a person couldn't find a River Rat if they tried was Rheth, capital city of Hallowspire, where were-rats, or any lycanthrope for that matter, was put to death like a diseased animal. Erasmus sat, wide-eyed at the situation, and noticing the subtle shifts of Lannister's bodyguards, motioned his own hand to the hilt of his short sword. No one spoke; O'doc barely allowed himself to breathe. Lannister's eyes narrowed, and a wide, disgusting smile formed on his face.

"I always knew you were the brains of this outfit, Lambkins."

Lannister Ravenclaw let out a great, sickly laugh as he motioned to one of his bodyguards to go gather the three hundred piece down-payment, and went on to order the group a round of drinks, discussing the details of the job at length.

O'doc spent the rest of the meeting trying his hardest not to pass out from relief.

CHAPTER TWO

Enna sat, cross-legged, eyes closed, in a small wooded patch. She had been sent to gather firewood, as she often had. As a young girl, she very much disliked the chore, as it meant having to occasionally trounce through the mud and muck to reach the wooded patch where the logs were kept, though as she grew older she found a sense of tranquility in the task. The feeling was something ineffable, a kind of peaceful familiarity brought about by something wholly unfamiliar. It was a feeling that Enna, especially as of late, began to relish.

And so, there she sat, cross-legged, eyes closed, feeling a light breeze cause her long auburn hair to play across her shoulders. The harvest had come and gone, and so she concentrated hard on that ineffable feeling, as it tended to wax and wane through the year. Enna felt it strongest during the midpoint of each season, and most consistently during the summer months. Now, during Autumn's final weeks, was when Enna had to begin really concentrating to tap into that feeling. She focused, long and hard, seeing in her mind's eye the faintest point of light in the distance. The light was not piercing, but warm and welcoming. Pushing her mind ever closer, she began to make out shapes within the light; dim, fuzzy shapes, but shapes nonetheless.

Clenching her teeth, curling her hands into fists, Enna tried to bring the shapes in her mind into focus. Gradually, the image of the shapes began to sharpen. They were foreign, something Enna could not begin to recognize, and yet she knew it was in her own mind that she saw them. The shapes emanated the same ineffable familiarity as the wooded patch where she sat, but there was something inherently stronger, more tangible about them. The shapes meant something, and as such were meant to convey something. Enna felt something unnatural within these shapes, and felt within herself an odd compulsion; to give these shapes a voice through herself. She drew in a deep breath, not knowing what words would come forth, but knowing very intrinsically how those words would feel, the shape her mouth and tongue would make to form them, and the cadence and intonation that would give those unknown words sound.

In the fraction of a moment before Enna could bring those words forth, she heard a voice in the distance, and her concentration was broken. "Enna!" her mother called from across the way "Enna Summerlark, if you don't get back inside with some wood, you and your father will be going to town with no more than a slice of day-old bread for each of ye!"

Enna let forth a heavy sigh, knowing well that it would be a long while until she could summon the time and concentration to get that close to those shapes in her mind again. For now, though, her mother was right: that day-old bread was in need of a stew, and the hearth was not going to burst into flame of its own accord. With a second, smaller sigh, Enna stood up, dusted herself off, gathered some firewood, and walked back toward her home.

***

Tessa Summerlark walked back into the quaint farmhouse that she and her husband Randis had called home for the past thirty years. Randis stood at the kitchen table, readying one of the many packs of goods for the day's trip. The weekly trips into town were something that he always looked forward to, as they were the closest he came to reliving his bygone mercantile days. Ever since the fateful night twenty years ago, when Enna had come into he and his wife's world, Randis forsook the road in favour of being ever-present for his new daughter, knowing that the less worldly he made himself, the less worldly Enna would want to be, and the safer she would be as a result. While Randis never once regretted his decision, he was a man of the road, and any man of the road will no doubt suffer some wanderlust when in one place for too long. As such, Randis' weekly excursions served as much as a way to save some extra coin as they did to save the man's sanity.

Tessa watched as her husband packed his things, neither saying much. Randis looked up, noticing a look on her face that had become almost ritualistic during market day. "Four years, now, Tess." he said with a half-smile peeking through his salt-and-pepper beard. "Four years I've been takin' the lass with me on market day, and never so much as a raised eyebrow." He walked towards her, taking her in his arms "So quit yer worryin', else that face'll wrinkle up like the squash I got hitched up to sell." Tessa hit her husband's broad chest playfully, then turned to help him pack.

"I know nothing's happened ever," she began while gathering eggs into a travel-safe basket, "and the Gods be thanked for that, but that doesn't stop me from worrying, Randis. Enna's a smart girl, and there's no doubt she's going to start noticing things, provided she hasn't already, and how long then?"

"How long 'til what?" Enna had caught only the last few words her mother had said as she slipped into the kitchen, placing the wood in the hearth underneath a large pot full of yet-to-be-cooked stew, and proceeding to reach for some flint.

"'Til the next traders' caravan arrives in town." Randis answered quickly. "Yer Mum was hoping I'd get some Braashine malachite to put 'round the house come winter."

"Braashre, that's one of the dwarven cities to the south, isn't it?" Enna asked, struggling with the flint.

"Aye, it is..." Randis said, a hint of nostalgia in his voice. "Beautiful cities the dwarves have. Finer stone and smith work than you'll see anywhere else."

"I never understood why you gave up trading, Dad." Enna continued to struggle with the flint as she talked. "All those exotic places, and people, and things. Don't you ever miss it?"

It was not an uncommon question. Enna asked it often of her father, and as always, he gave the same reply. "There are plenty of beautiful and exotic things out there, lass..."

"But none as beautiful as you or your Mum." Tessa and Enna said in unison. Finally, there was a spark of flint, and flames began to lick about the wood. "I swear," Enna said, exasperated "one of these day's I'll find a way to start a fire without troubling myself with any stupid flint..." the girl giggled to herself at the thought, unbeknownst to her that it caused Tessa to give her husband a worried sidelong glance.

As the stew cooked, the rest of the preparations were made for the day. As Enna went out to help her father hitch the horses to the wagon, Tessa tapped her on the shoulder, prompting her to turn about-face. "Yes Mum?"

Tessa opened her hand, revealing a pair of silver ear cuffs. "Forgetting something?" Seeing her daughter's slightly incredulous look, she added "Come now, your father had them crafted specially for you, and he loves when you wear them, especially on market day."

Enna allowed a slight upward curl to reach the corner of her mouth. "Alright, alright... for Dad." she said, taking the cuffs and placing them over the tops of her ears, and in doing so covering the faintest hints of scarring that ran along the tops of both.

"Beautiful." Tessa said with a smile, brushing her daughter's hair aside, and giving her a kiss on the forehead. "Now off with ye, and keep an eye on your father's purse; he needs to save up for that malachite!"

Tessa watched as her husband and daughter headed off toward town, silently whispering a prayer, as she always did, asking the gods to keep them safe. She knew that one day she and Randis would have to answer all those unasked questions regarding Enna, and she worried not only that that day was fast approaching, but that the questions may not remain unasked for much longer.

CHAPTER THREE

A light autumnal rain was falling along the trade road heading east from Mossy Bluff. Erasmus and O'doc had been on the road for roughly three weeks, and in that time there had been three constants: the rain, the lack of available horses, and the pessimistic fretting of O'doc Overhill.

"This whole thing is ridiculous... ludicrous, inconceivably half-witted!"

"Don't forget," Erasmus added, jingling their coin purse "the best paying job we've ever worked. I still can't believe you convinced Lannister Ravenclaw to pay us a thousand gold crowns for this."

"*I* still can't believe Lannister Ravenclaw convinced *us* to go to *Hallowspire*, a kingdom where mortal folk have a hard enough time gaining entry." O'doc looked pointedly at his partner "never mind what they think of fae-folk!"

"*Half* fae-folk" Erasmus corrected with an equally pointed glare. "And don't worry, I'll keep my hood up and my head down."

"Be that as it may," the halfling continued, "provided we manage to get into the capital without any trouble, and provided we can *keep* out of trouble while we're there, we have to try and look for someone. Someone, I might add, who we have no information or leads on, *only* that he or she is roughly twenty years old, and an elf."

"So how hard can that be? Finding the only elf in the Great Bastion of Humanity?"

"If you were the only elf in the Great Bastion of Humanity," O'doc looked incredulously, "what lengths would you go to *not* to stick out?"

Erasmus didn't respond, but rather had his attention drawn toward the faint sound of bustle up ahead. "I think there's a caravan in the distance."

"Oh, good." O'doc replied, shaking the rainwater from his cloak "maybe they'll let us use their campfire for the night."

"And maybe," Erasmus added, a mischievous smirk playing on his face "they'll let us use one of their coaches for the rest of his trip."

O'doc could not help but smile and shake his head, knowing the look on Erasmus' face, and knowing that while the night's events had the potential to end with the pair walking the ever- darkening trade road in the rain, they also had the potential to end with a cushy coach ride the rest of the way to Hallowspire. Regardless of the outcome, however, O'doc was certain that the night would not be an uneventful one.

***

The fire at the caravan's campsite was friendly and welcoming. Erasmus Stonehand was anything but. This was not to say that he and O'doc were being overtly rude to the six men and one woman who had allowed them shelter for the night, but the half-elf's patience for his hosts was slowly diminishing.

Sitting semicircular around the opposite end of the fire were the occupants of the two wagons that formed the caravan. All appeared to be farmers and peasants, and five of the men were flanking the sixth, who had on his lap his newlywed bride. The men were raucously regaling stories of tavern brawls and sexual conquests, all the while the bride held the kind of smile indicative of someone who is not at all enjoying oneself.

"An' that..." the bridegroom slurred, waving his flagon about "is when I met this little hen. Yer see, her dad was about to come at me with a hatchet after he'd heard 'bout what I'd did with his other daughter..." his cohorts roared with drunken laughter while O'doc stared uncomfortably into his own untouched flagon and Erasmus smiled a polite, if completely disingenuous smile.

"But then I tells him 'wait, you don't know who I am!' Sure enough, soon as he finds out my uncle's the liege-lord what owns the very land he's standing on, he starts groveling! Damned fool was on th' brink of blubberin', telling me his daughter's all mine if I wants her fer a little wifey..." the following belch emitted by the groom was such that Erasmus would have sworn he saw the fire raise as a result.

"Get to the good part, Ogden," one of the other men spurned "'fore you pass out an' forget!"

"I'm getting to it, ye great ass!" Ogden turned and shouted, and then turned back to his guests "Sorry. So, I tells the poor bugger, I don't want that daughter fer a wife, 'cause she ain't a virgin anymore!" More inebriated laughter ensued. "So, then, he shows me this little hen, tells me she's not never known a man." he pinched her cheek with lecherous affection. "She ain't the prettiest, but I'll tell you what, she's prettier'n Dougan's sister!"

One man, presumably Dougan, laughed and gestured vulgarly at Ogden. Another of the men, presumably not Dougan, spoke up. "Oi! That's my wife yer saying that about!"

Another of the men, presumably neither Dougan nor his brother-in-law, piped in. "Aw please, Jeres, your wife couldn't get a pig to kiss 'er if she was covered in shit... and the Gods know she's tried!"

Through the laughter, Erasmus stood up and cleared his throat. He reached into his pack, and pulled out his mandolin. "Gentlemen, milady," he said, subtly winking at O'doc, "can I interest you in a song?"

The men began to cheer and call out requests.

"Play the one about the Whore of Pheasantkeep!"

"No, the one about the man what caught his wife with another man an' then got 'imself another wife!"

"I was thinking," Erasmus raised a silencing hand "Something a bit more...dulcet."

And with that, Erasmus began to pluck softly at the stings of his mandolin, and sing, in a rough- hewn tenor, a lullaby.

Rest ye now child, 'tis end of the day,
The moon in the sky and the fae-folk at play,
For if you should wake 'fore the sunlight should break
Then the pixies and wisps shall spirit y'way.

Rest ye now child, though 'tis warm this night,
Calling through veils every satyr and sprite,
For if you make a sound while there's fae-folk around,
Then I shall never again have your face in my sight.

Erasmus never knew the origin of the tune, past it being one his mother taught him in his youth, and had yet to meet anyone else who even knew it. As his fingers plucked the strings and danced across the instrument's neck, he kept note of his audience, who had begun to grow quiet and still. Erasmus continued into the second verse amid the captive group, the lyrics changing from the Common tongue to Elvish.

Come with me child, for there's much you could see,
I'll teach you to dance among river and tree,
Be not filled with fear as I beckon you near
For the Fae offer but jollity and glee.

Come with me child, 'fore the start of the day,
My voice you will follow without pause or delay,
So look deep in my eyes whilst the moon rules the skies,
And know the Kingdom of Wood has you in its sway.

As Erasmus finished the tune, he was pleased to see six sets of glazed eyes staring at him with vacant attentiveness. He looked to O'doc and nodded, to which the halfling responded by removing the bits of wax he had discreetly placed in his ears before Erasmus had begun his performance. "Gentlemen," Erasmus announced "I think, perhaps, you all ought to sleep, and forget this night."

The five men, needing no further prompting, and making not a sound, obliged the request, curling up around the fire. O'doc let loose a small chuckle and shook his head. "The bumpkins are always your best crowds."

"Simple minds." Erasmus said plainly. "Now, old friend, if you'd be so kind as to help me bind their hands and feet."

"And their coin?"

"Relieve them of it; swine have little use for gold."

As the two went swiftly about their task, O'doc motioned to the woman, still sitting silently, staring blankly. "And her? We can't well send her back to her hometown."

Erasmus nodded, and pursed his lips a moment in concentration. He strode over to the woman and looked into her eyes. "Milady, tell me your name."

"Nell." the woman responded flatly. "Nell Ashwood."

"Nell," Erasmus said, still looking into her eyes, "come dawn, you will take one of these wagons and ride it to East Fellowdale. When you reach East Fellowdale, you will go to a tavern called The Merchant's Den. You will ask for the owner, a halfling named Orne Raftmite. Tell him that Erasmus Stonehand sent you, with regards, and he will give you a room and a job." He looked to O'doc, who was in the process of counting the coins he'd taken from the sleeping men. "How much?"

"Less than you'd expect from a Lord's nephew and his cronies..." he mused. "Twenty five crowns and twelve coppers, all in all."

"Pass it over." Erasmus held out his hand.

"What? But..."

"But nothing. We have plenty of our down payment left, and you can bet some of that was this poor creature's to begin with."

O'doc gave the resigned huff of someone who knew he'd been beaten by logic, slid the coins into one of the purses, and gave it to Erasmus, who then placed it into Nell's hands, and looked back into her eyes. "At dawn, you ride for East Fellowdale and begin your life anew, do you understand?" Nell slowly nodded.

"Good. And now, off to sleep with you." Erasmus took the woman by the hand and started to lead her away from the fire, toward the tents pitched between the wagons.

O'doc looked at his partner disapprovingly. "So I imagine I'll be taking first watch then?"

"Don't be ridiculous." Erasmus countered defensively. "If I want to charm a woman into my bed, I can do so without arcana, thank you very much." Erasmus led the woman to a tent, and when she climbed inside, he turned to O'doc. "Besides, we've not got any time to play. We have to leave."

"Now? In the dead of night?"

"Of course." Erasmus said, untying one of the caravan horses from a nearby tree. "With a wagon, if we leave now, we could make it to Hallowspire by midday tomorrow."

"Fine enough," O'doc said as he gathered his belongings, "but seeing as this is your idea, first shift driving is yours. All this excitement has tired me right out!"

CHAPTER FOUR

Lannister Ravenclaw strode through the streets of Delverbrook. There was a confidence in the halfling's gait; this was his town. Prior to Ravenclaw's tenure as guildmaster, the River Rats were a third-tier band of burglars, at best. In the last five years, however, the halfling had reorganized the Rats from the ground up. There was resistance, of course; if not from the guild's old guard, than from rival guilds who knew the changes would upset the established hierarchy. No, the changes did not come easily for the Rats, or for Ravenclaw, but then scant little had ever been easy for Lannister Ravenclaw. Much akin to the rats with whom he held a lycanthropic bond, the halfling was a survivor, a simple urchin who spent too many years sneaking, scavenging, and eventually clawing his way to the top. Yes, after all the time and struggle, this was Lannister Ravenclaw's town, and he had no trouble letting anyone know that. It was with such an evident air of pomp that the halfling sauntered down a side street in one of Delverbrook's more affluent corners, to a small, nondescript building with two robed, hooded men standing on either side of the door.

"You are late, Guildmaster." the man on the left stated blankly, retaining his stoic position.

"I had other business." Ravenclaw snapped. "Your boss isn't my only client, and he'd do well to remember that."

"The Master has concerns of his own," the man on the right said with a similar flatness. "Concerns of much greater import." He, too, stood unflinching.

"Your 'master'" Lannister snapped with indignation "can think whatever he likes of his time and affairs, and if he has some kind of problem, he can tell me himself. I'll not be threatened by the two waifs he likely pays two bit a week to stand around in front of a door!"

The two robed men stood, silent and unmoving. After a moment, Lannister shook his head, let out a disgusted sigh, and swung the doors to the building open. As he started to enter, the man to the left spoke in a slow monotone. "This was not a threat."

"Merely a reminder" the man on the right continued similarly "of the Master's vast, if waning patience." Lannister stood for a moment, looking at the unflinching men flanking him, only to shake his head and continue through the entrance.

The doors closed behind the halfling, leaving little light, as no lamps or torches were evident. Standing for a moment in the darkness, Lannister took a deep breath and concentrated. He felt the familiar tingle run up down and across his skin, felt the muscles throughout his body begin to reshape, expanding some features, contracting others, and altering some altogether. Now came the tricky part of it, a technique that took many lycanthropes years, even decades to master. The halfling, fighting every involuntary movement in his body, began to slow his transformation. His head throbbed, and he winced, as this technique was never a painless one. Finally, after several excruciating minutes, Lannister opened his eyes and, rather than seeing only blackness, he could see through the pitch black hallway as though it were no darker than an open field on a clear night. His clothes were hanging slightly looser than before; he had yet to figure out how to halt the shrinking aspect of the transformation. Still, looking forward, the now small-halfling-sized bipedal rat saw a set of stone stairs descending below the building, and proceeded to scurry down them.

The stairs descended in a wide spiral several tens of feet below, where at their base stood a large wood door bearing a brass sigil that, Lannister had surmised, was the symbol of this arcane order, or temple, or whatever exactly it was. Pushing the door open, the were-rat strode into a large antechamber, walls lined ceiling to floor with old tomes that gave the room an antique, musty scent. Several men and women of varying ages and races, all wearing robes similar to those worn by the men out front, dotted the large chamber. Some perused the archaic stacks, some sat at plain wood tables, either reading one of the old tomes or scratching things down on sheets of parchment. There was an odd stillness about the room that Lannister found off-putting the few times he had come here; never mind the fact that the halfling was inherently more accustomed to the busyness of urban bustle, there was something lacking from the movements of the robed figures in the room that one might otherwise sense in a monastery or arcane university. There was something, Lannister felt that was so methodical in the movements of these robed individuals that it was almost unnatural. Lannister shrugged off his unease and strode to the far end of the chamber, not a single robed figure taking notice of his presence. At the chamber's far end there stood another door, large and plain, and bearing the same brass sigil as the door leading in. Relaxing his mind, and therein returning to his natural form, Lannister Ravenclaw pulled open the door and entered.

The room on the other side of the door was well lit, though not by candle or torch. Rather, at the four corners of the room and at its centre stood tall ornate candlesticks, each holding a crystalline orb. All of the orbs, save the one in the centre of the room, were glowing with a soft white light that illuminated the small room as though by natural sunlight. At either side of the centremost candlestick, facing the door and the back wall, were two plain stone daises. With a deep breath, Lannister stepped onto the dais on the side of the door, and waited. After a moment, the temperature in the room began to drop, and the orbs in each corner began to glow with an intensity several times greater than when the halfling had entered. Once the bright light had become almost unbearable, streams of the blinding luminescence shot from each orb in the form of four concentrated beams, all converging on the centre orb. This caused the centre orb to begin illuminating, and the surrounding orbs to dim to a more bearable level. The centre orb reached a critical brightness similar to those in the corners, but rather than expelling the energy as a concentrated beam, it shone outward toward the unoccupied dais. The light from the centre orb shone a crude, fuzzy shape at first, but quickly sharpened, revealing the ghostly life-sized image of a tall figure in robes similar to the occupants of the building, but with an ornateness to them to signify a much higher station.

"Guildmaster Ravenclaw," the simulacrum said in a distant, spectral voice. "I trust that your tardiness to this meeting was in some way related to our Mission?" The image was not so well defined that one could make out the facial features under the cowl, and as such Lannister saw only a fuzzy darkness where a face ought to be.

"My time spent prior to coming here is *my* business." Lannister sneered "But rest assured my good man, *our* business is being handled."

"You have found individuals for the task, then?" the image asked with little change in its tone.

"Two of the best." Lannister answered with smug pride "They're on the road as we speak, and if I know them as well as I ought to, they'll be in and out faster than anyone'll expect."

"Good. Time grows ever shorter in this matter, and the elf has hid itself well. If these individuals are as competent as you boast, you will be rewarded handsomely." The image's voice was monotonous, devoid of anything Lannister might use to read whether or not its claims were genuine, and yet the idea of the rewards that had previously been discussed could not help but cause him to grin greedily.

"I assure you," the halfling smiled "your faith in the Rats, and in myself, will not go unfounded."

"Excellent." the image said stoically. "Now, Guildmaster Ravenclaw, one final matter: thrice now have you come to meet here, and thrice have you allowed other matters to delay your arrival..."

"Now look, I told you..." the halfling's protest was cut short by a searing pain he felt emerge beneath the skin of his left shoulder.

"Any excuses are unacceptable." the image stated. "Our Mission is paramount to all others, and as such, it is necessary that you exercise the utmost punctuality." Lannister winced and fell to one knee, pulling at his jacket and shirt to reveal what looked like a brand emerging from below his skin. "This mark is a blessing; all with it know intrinsically of all others with it. This mark can, however, be a curse; failure to follow our Mission in a timely manner will result in consequences..." With that, the orb in the centre of the room glowed bright and intense, reaching its climax in a flash that mirrored the pain of Lannister, causing him to double over and fall off the dais. In an instant, the simulacrum was gone, the centre orb was dark, and the room was as it had been when the halfling had entered. Looking at his shoulder, he saw burned into his flesh that same sigil on the doors, still hot to the touch.

The halfling collected himself and opened the door back

into the antechamber. Gone was the controlled methodical silence of the robed figures in the chamber; replaced now with the eerie still of several sets unblinking of eyes turned, staring directly at him. Lannister walked quickly across the chamber to the exit, his walk now hurried and uncomfortable. He kept his gaze ever ahead, knowing the whole time that all those unblinking eyes were on them, and wanting anything but to meet their gaze. He hurried out the door and slammed it shut, fumbling his way up the stone steps and along the stone corridor in pitch blackness before reaching the building's exit.

Lannister Ravenclaw ran through the streets of Delverbrook, all confidence gone from his step.

CHAPTER FIVE

Enna sat next to her father as the wagon rolled along the dirt road to Rheth. The capital city was not so far that the weekly excursions were a great inconvenience, but the distance was substantial enough that it took a solid four hours one way in ideal weather. In the last four years the pair had made the trip, the nature of how they passed the time while on the road had changed gradually. When Enna was younger, Randis made a point of doing what he could to keep his daughter entertained. Over the years, as the excursion became more and more routine, the need to fill the trip with hours of oftentimes forced conversation dwindled. Now when the two talked they did so comfortably, and when the two sat in silence they did so comfortably as well. Currently, the latter was the case, and while Randis was at the horses' reigns, Enna sat thinking. Remembering.

She thought back to when she was much younger, about ten or eleven. Her family had gone to Rheth that market day as an excursion. It was one of the few times at that point that Enna had been to the capital, when the sights and sounds and smells were all still fresh. She remembered being overwhelmed by the colossal front gates; great doors of wood and iron that were taller even than her house, and straight-faced guards in shiny plate armour that greeted their wagon; one guard asked her father questions, while the other looked through the wagon. Once the men were finished, they called to more guards atop the great gate and the doors slowly opened.

The city's interior was much like the smaller towns in Hallowspire that Enna had visited up to that point; people lined the streets, many with carts or booths set up selling all manner of things. The family found an empty spot for their wagon next to a young halfling couple, who were likely from Summershore to the south judging by the river fish they were selling. Enna helped her parents set up the wagon as best she could, gathering produce and laying it out for display, and when everything was set Enna's father stayed to sell while she and her mother went to explore the market.

There were two things about Rheth that made it feel different from the other cities Enna had visited in Hallowspire. First, was its sheer magnitude; most of the cities in the kingdom had large town halls, one or two taverns, and a fair number of shops. The larger ones had keeps, numerous inns, and entire sections devoted not only to shops, but to the people who lived within the city walls. Rheth, however, dwarfed all the others by comparison. The castle alone, the great stone structure at Rheth's centre, had grounds that spanned further than the entire area of the smaller cities. Its central spire, a tower that rose so tall that Enna was certain that anyone standing at its peak could see to the edges of the kingdom.

The other thing that differentiated Rheth from the other cities in the kingdom was the presence of the King's Guard. Similar to the guards out front at the city gate, they were adorned with shining plate armour, holding a pike in one hand and a large shield with the King's crest in the other. The guard were not unique in appearance, however; rather it was the sheer volume of guards throughout the city. Indeed one could not move from one street to the next without seeing at least one of the Guard patrolling it. Most were friendly enough, nodding to passersby; a few even said hello to Enna on occasion. When she was much younger, Enna had never noticed, nor paid much mind to the constant presence of the guard. It was on that day, she remembered, that their presence began to seem odd.

"Mum," she looked up to her mother "why are there so many King's Guard around Rheth?"

"Well, sweet," her mother had answered "do you remember when your father and I first started to teach you about the Four Kingdoms?"

Enna nodded. "Yes mum: Hallowspire, Lohvast, Majadrin, and Ghest."

"That's right, and who rules the Four Kingdoms?"

"The Kings, of course!" Enna thought a moment, "Oh, and the

Queen in Lohvast."

"And who, besides the Kings and Queen," her mother had continued "are the most powerful individuals in the Kingdoms?"

Enna pondered slightly on this one "The...archer mages? The ones who know the best magic."

"The Archmages." her mother corrected "And yes, sweet, they are very powerful arcanists."

Enna looked down thoughtfully, trying to piece together the conversation. "So... what do the Archmages have to do with all the King's Guard?"

"Well, think about it; the most powerful people who aren't royals are arcanists. That means that arcanists must be very powerful." Enna nodded, following her mother's logic. "So sweet, tell me: if you were queen of Hallowspire, would you want lots of people around who were that powerful?"

"Sure, why not?"

"Because what if two, or five, or even ten of those people decided that they didn't like you?"

"Why wouldn't they like me? They've never even met me!"

"Maybe they think they could do a better job ruling Hallowspire." Enna's mother offered. "Now suppose you had all these very powerful people, would you feel safe knowing that they could come after you and you would be almost totally helpless?"

"So... the King's Guard make sure that no arcanists go after the king?"

"Exactly. In fact, they make sure that no one in the kingdom, especially in Rheth, even practices arcana without the proper permission from the Archmage."

From there, Enna's memory jumped ahead, to she and her mother going down one of Rheth's winding cobblestone streets, to where several artisan tents sold all manner of handcrafted goods, Commonalities and oddities in equal measure. Enna's mother had her attention on a tent where an older woman was selling bolts of wool and strings of glass beads, when Enna heard a low, hearty voice from behind them.

"Fine crystal or stonework for the two lovely ladies?"

Enna looked over to see a stout, bearded man, no taller than she, with striking violet eyes, dark hair and pale skin. "You're a dwarf!" she said in an excited whisper.

"Enna Summerlark, your manners!" Her mother turned to face the dwarf "I'm sorry, my daughter didn't mean to offend; not many dwarves make their way through Hallowspire."

"Ahh, it's nothing" the dwarf shrugged, then tipped his hat, and gave a slight bow. "Adrik Thornmallet, at miladies' service." Adrik gave young Enna a wink, causing her to giggle.

Enna's mother admired the wares in the dwarf's tent "Your pieces are gorgeous, Master Thornmallet."

"Adrik will do just fine," he responded "if it please milady."

"Oh, my manners!" Enna's mother blushed "Tessa Summerlark, and this is my daughter Enna."

"What fine names!" Adrik grinned through his black braided beard "Enna..." he turned to her "that's an elven name, if I'm not mistaken."

Enna nodded excitedly "Yes sir, my dad said he heard it once while he was a merchant, and that he thought it was the prettiest name, so he was gonna give it to the prettiest girl."

"Well," Adrik let out a bellowing chuckle "your dad sounds like a smart man with a good eye for beauty. If I weren't so wise, I'd think he'd have plucked you from the fae-folk with his bare hands!"

Enna shared a laugh with the dwarf "That's silly; there's no fae-folk in Hallowspire! Right mum?"

"That's right, sweet." Enna's mother smiled politely at the dwarf.

"Well, I'll tell you what," Adrik ducked behind his display and began to rummage. "I think I've got just the pieces here..." He emerged with a dainty jade bracelet adorned with dwarven lettering, and a thin leather necklace with a small quartz pendant dangling from it.

Enna's eyes widened as she looked at jewelry. "Oh, mum, they're so pretty!"

Enna's mother pursed her lips contemplatively "They are very lovely..." she said to Adrik.

"For miladies, a piece and three." the dwarf offered with a grin.

"That little?" Enna's mother said in disbelief "Master Thornmallet, I..."

"Adrik, please"

"Adrik..." she continued "that is very generous, but these materials... surely we'd be taking advantage of you..."

"Nonsense!" Adrik waved his hand dismissively. "Where I come from I could throw a rock and hit a finer rock, and that first rock'd be precious to begin with!" He let out another guffaw "Trust me, my offer is more than fair for everyone. All I ask is that whenever you happen to be here for market day, you come look for old Adrik and say hello." He turned to Enna "And make sure you wear one of these pieces so I know who it is when some beautiful young woman comes to greet me; happens so little I might otherwise get confused."

Enna put her hand to her mouth to cover the fact that she was blushing, and looked up at her mother hopefully. "Well, alright." her mother said after a moment, reaching into her coin purse to pay the dwarf "but keep the pieces in your bag, sweet, so you can show them to your father." Enna did so. The pair thanked the dwarf and went about their day.

Enna's memory now drifted past the rest of the day spent in Rheth, and to that night, when she snuck out of her bedroom to collect the pendant she had left in the kitchen, when she heard her parents talking.

"I'm telling you, Randis, he knew something."

"Well, I'm not saying that it's impossible, Tess. He wouldn't have been from around here; he'd know the look, he'd have seen them often enough to know."

"So why aren't you worried?"

"Because this is Hallowspire. King Renton would sooner work the local men and women halfway to death before he'd ask for help outside the kingdom."

"Maybe you're right... I just worry..."

By this point, Enna knew the conversation wasn't going to end anytime soon, just as she knew she would be in trouble for being out of bed this late. She went back to bed, and when she awoke the quartz pendant on the leather necklace was sitting on her bedside table.

After that, Enna went to market day only once before she turned sixteen, when she began to go to help her father. Every trip she wore the pendant, hoping to see Adrik. By the time she turned eighteen she no longer expected that she may one day reunite with the jovial dwarf from her childhood. She still wore the pendant on market day, though mostly out of habit; it was a lovely pendant, after all.

"Y'know," Randis said to Enna, pulling her back from her memories "Your mum almost didn't want you to keep that thing." He had caught Enna twirling the pendant idly, as she often did without knowing.

"Well, I'm glad she did," Enna smiled back "It's still so pretty, and it reminds me of a great day."

The two continued on in comfortable silence until reaching the main gates into Rheth.

CHAPTER SIX

It was midday. A nondescript wagon lumbered toward the main gates of Rheth, driven by a halfling who did not own it, and whose companion, a half-elf, was doing his best to keep a hood over his slightly pointed ears without looking altogether suspicious.

"Are you sure this is how you want to do this?"

"Absolutely. We do it this way, we'll draw far less attention to ourselves."

"You could hide in the back, perhaps in one of the trunks?"

"Thieves call this city the million-eyed monster for a reason, O'doc; better I hide in plain sight."

"If you say so. Just make sure you've got on your best lying face, and by all the Gods, please don't use that mandolin."

"Oh, don't fret," Erasmus said both reassuringly and begrudgingly "Caster's safely tucked away in her case."

As the two rolled close to the gate, they were flagged down by one of the two King's Guard standing at either side. O'doc pulled the reigns, stopping the horses. "Names." the larger Guard said. O'doc's quick eyes allowed him to notice a ledger being held by said Guard, with a list of names, some checked, some unchecked. A cursory glance allowed him to find two appropriate, unchecked names. "Garret Blacktrout, and Redgar Quinn."

"Blacktrout and Quinn?" the smaller Guard said in the voice indicative of a female. "Those two are twice the age of these men!"

The larger guard stood imposing over O'doc. "Names. Real names or I call on the archers up in the turrets to let loose a score of crossbow bolts into each of you!"

"We're not Blacktrout and Quinn," Erasmus said in an apologetic tone, turning to the female Guard. "Not Garret and Redgar, anyway. In truth, he is Ulmo Blacktrout and I am Brigg Quinn. Our fathers were not feeling well this morning, and asked us to head to Rheth in their stead. They did say they would bring the spare wagon and meet us later, provided they had it in them."

"Blacktrout and Quinn have never mentioned sons..." the male Guard stammered.

"Well, perhaps they don't feel like sharing their home lives when you speak to them in such a tone!" O'doc chastised him. "It's no wonder dad always comes home in such a state. I've been going to Rheth since before you were born, and still they talk to me like I'm some gibbering babe that needs his ass wiped!' he'll say, well now I can say I can't blame him in the least." O'doc shifted in the seat of the wagon, turning his face forward in mock disgust of the male Guard.

"Please," Erasmus gave the female Guard his best desperate eyes. "If we wait for our fathers, we'll be out half a day's earnings, provided they even show up."

The female guard paused a moment. "Let them in!" she called to the gate tower "All clear, let them in!" The sound of gears and pulleys followed as the large gate raised up, allowing the wagon to roll into the streets of Rheth.

"As I said last night," Erasmus whispered to his partner as they crossed the threshold into the capital city, "No arcana necessary."

The streets were lined up and down with wagons and tents, all manner of sights sounds and smells filling them. "I guess it's market day." O'doc mused "That'll make it that much harder to find our target."

"True," Erasmus said, "but look on the bright side: we have trunks full of a noble-born brat's clothes, and streets filled with potential buyers. If worse comes to worse, we can at least make a bit more coin to cover somewhere to stay." Erasmus scanned the area as they rolled down the cobblestone. "There." he pointed "That seems like a fair spot to set up shop."

The halfling pulled the wagon into an empty space between an older human selling whittled wooden animals and a halfling family selling fresh baked goods. While O'doc tied the horse up to a nearby post, Erasmus unpacked the stolen trunks, sitting them empty at street side to act as makeshift display tables. He went through the stolen clothes, which varied from plain and practical to opulent and gaudy. Gathering up what he deemed salable, Erasmus took the clothes, armful by armful, and lay them out on the trunks to be displayed. When the makeshift display was covered, the half-elf's bardic nature set in. "Ladies and Gentlemen," he crooned "come feast your eyes upon some of the finest cut clothes in all the Four Kingdoms. Cottons so soft that Queen Merrian of Lohvast demands them for her bedsheets. Wools so warm that farmers could harvest through winter, if the Gods allowed anything to grow. Silks dyed in colours so vibrant that the dwarves are envious that their finest gem work does not shine as bright!"

"So, please Erasmus, explain to me," O'doc asked as Erasmus continued his performance "How is this going to help us find what we're looking for?"

"For one thing, *Ulmo*, blending." Erasmus said over his shoulder. "Yes sir, brand new, you might as well be wearing the sheep." the half-elf pocketed some coin "We look like we ought to be here, keeps people's guards down. Of course, milady, one size fits most!" more coin. "Not to mention, the busyness of today means this may take us more than one day. A shame, my good man, your loss! And I, for one, would like to spend the night in a soft bed for a change."

O'doc nodded reservedly "I suppose you're right....*Brigg*, but remember, no performances outside of this little sales pitch."

"Swear by the Gods, she's still packed in the wagon. A mere five for these pantaloons, madame? Your sense of humour has brightened my day; I'll drop the price to seven, just for you."

O'doc shook his head and gave a reserved smile, walked back to the wagon and got a small stool out of the back. Setting it down on the opposite side of the trunks from his partner, he stood atop it, and began to bellow as loud as he could. "Step right up, Masters and Maidens, come and feel the finest clothes from here to Ghest!"

CHAPTER SEVEN

igh in one of the tallest rooms in the central spire of the castle at the heart of Rheth, King Renton Isevahr stood looking over his capital city. The king was not old, nor was he terribly young, but for all he had seen and experienced in the last thirty years, he felt himself quite wise beyond his years. Indeed, by forty-two, most of the royals in the history of the Four Kingdoms had a decade of the title king or queen under their belts, at best. Many had, by Renton's age, married and had young princes and princesses before ascending to the throne. Few had ascended as a result of the brutal assassination of the incumbent king, and fewer still had to cope with the assassination of the incumbent queen as well. Barely any had to live six years as a king answering to not one, but two different Archmages, and none had affected the kind of drastic change in their kingdoms Renton had as a result. Yes, King Renton Isevahr felt his wisdom was indeed far beyond his years, and he felt his kingdom was all the better for it.

His thoughts were interrupted by the sound of footsteps approaching him. "These are good times for Hallowspire, Archmage Tyn." He turned to face a slight looking man in flowing crimson robes emblazoned with the crest of Hallowspire. The King smiled through his gray-tipped beard "Derrus," he addressed the Archmage more colloquially "I trust all is well on the streets today?"

"Of course, your Grace," the robed man said with a low, reverent bow. "This month's market day has been, as ever, free of incident. The people of Hallowspire are enjoying the fruits of one another's labour, without worry of the kind of hooliganism and unrest that plagues their neighbours in the rest of the Four Kingdoms."

The King turned back to his view of the capital city, and nodded.

"It has been the right course of action we've taken all these years, has it not? We have had to make some drastic decisions over the years..."

"*You*, your Grace," the Archmage walked up to stand next to the King "have had to make many a decision whilst faced with all manner of adversity. Such responsibility would have crushed a lesser man, suffocated him underneath its magnitude." He lay a hand on the King's shoulder. "You have made difficult decisions, yes, but look out at your city, your kingdom, your *people*, your Grace. The people of Hallowspire may be without certain frivolities, yes, but they have peace, and they have happiness. *You* gave them that, your Grace, and they adore you for it. You honour your parents, and I have every faith that were they able to see what you have accomplished, they would be proud."

Renton turned his head and smiled at the Archmage "Thank you, Derrus. You are truly a good friend. I could not have received a better adviser or Archmage had the Gods themselves delivered me one."

"You flatter me." the Archmage waved away the compliment. "After the debacle with your last Archmage a drooling goblin wrapped in a bolt of silk would have been an improvement."

The King pursed his lips "Yes, I prefer not to dwell on such dark spots." The pair turned and began to talk toward the doors. "So Derrus, do tell: how has your correspondence with the Archmage of Lohvast been progressing?"

"On some topics, your Grace, I have made little headway. For instance, Archmage Elbar continues to remain resolute on the matter of keeping the Arcane University's policies as they are; he refuses to see the danger in keeping admittance public and free for all who possess a talent in Arcana."

"The fools." the king responded "Such lackadaisical handling of that kind of power will reduce Queen Merrian's lands and people to chaos."

"My thoughts exactly. Now, on the subject of her Grace..."

"No, Derrus."

"Your Grace, I had not yet..."

"Not yet what, Derrus? Attempted to talk up the Queen of Lohvast to me like some farmer anxious to be rid of a spinster daughter?"

"Your Grace, consider: Though she is unmarried, and has

been on the Lohvastine throne for just shy of a decade, she is still of childbearing age, and the unification of Lohvast and Hallowspire would be monumental. Archmage Elbar has assured me that her Grace is a lovely woman."

"And I have heard tell that she is arrogant and flighty." the King retorted.

"Think of the potential for peace, your Grace. Your marrying Queen Merrian could result in a complete transformation of Lohvast. You and she, your Grace, could go down in history as the great pacifiers of the Four Kingdoms."

The King considered this a moment, stroking his short, well-kept beard contemplatively. "No." he said with finality. "There is still much work to be done in Lohvast before I would even consider opening our gates to them. When the Queen and Archmage Elbar have begun to realize the disaster they are heading toward, and begin making efforts to rectify it, then *perhaps* I will consider greater correspondence between our kingdoms."

"A wise decision." the Archmage bowed low. "I shall redouble my efforts in convincing Archmage Elbar to enact change for the better of Lohvast."

"See that you do." the king nodded "You are dismissed, Archmage Tyn."

With a final bow, the Archmage excused himself, leaving the King to return to his silent vigil over his capital city. Derrus had been right on one account; the King was not getting any younger, and largely due to his own stubbornness, had yet to produce an heir. What would happen to his kingdom after he passed? Chaos, likely; political and social unrest, the destruction of everything he had spent the better part of his life working toward, everything his parents had died for. The King closed his eyes and shuddered at the thought.

CHAPTER EIGHT

Enna and Randis Summerlark were situated in their regular section of one of the main streets, a small wooden display set up with all manner of seasonal goods; potatoes, all manner of gourds, various jars of preserves that Tessa had prepared in the weeks prior. Enna watched her father work the crowd, something that never failed to amaze her. Randis was a loving and doting father and husband, and an affable man to his neighbours, but come market day something awakened within him. Randis had, as Enna well knew, been a well-traveled merchant before she was born. At home, his years on the road seemed buried deep under the layers of a toiling farmer. Once a month, however, the people in Rheth saw the man that lay beneath those layers, the man who had traded with dwarven thanes, who provided the arcane universities with their harder-to-procure components, and who could bottle fireflies and sell them as pixies for fifty pieces each, were he not so honest.

For the most part, Enna allowed her father to work the crowd while she gathered and counted the coin, packed the sold goods for patrons, and smiled with a genuine thanks for their business. In recent years, Enna would occasionally draw the attention of young men, who she would often had to inform that she was not for sale, or that no, a kiss would not be sufficient payment for anything that *was* for sale. While Enna had become increasingly used to these kinds of occurrences, to the point where they were the equivalent of swatting away bothersome horseflies, she feared for whichever tactless would-be suitor was caught in the act by her father, who even though he was quickly approaching fifty years of age still cut an imposing figure.

By early afternoon, as was custom on market day, there was a lull that afforded all the sellers some time to eat, and to peruse one another's carts and stands. For many, market day was as much about selling one's goods as it was about looking for goods that were not readily available to oneself. Enna and Randis ran chunks of bread through the thick stew prepared that morning, and took stock of what had been and had yet-to-be sold. Randis, who had worked up an appetite with his performance, devoured his portion, stood up, and stretched his muscles. "Think ye can manage things a few moments?" he asked Enna "I ought to go look for that malachite, else your mum'll be fit to tear when we get back."

"Go ahead, Dad." Enna answered, chewing. "I'll make sure no one tries to short change us."

"Keep up talkin' with your mouth full 'o stew and we'll be lucky if anyone even wants to buy our goods." Randis jokingly chastised, prompting Enna to hold her hand up to her mouth with an embarrassed smile. "Be good now, I'll not be long." Enna nodded and finished her mouthful as her father walked off into the streets of Rheth.

Enna sat, finishing her stew while she took in the sights. True, Rheth did not have the novel appeal it held for Enna as a child, but it was still immense, and even after coming to the city monthly for the last four years, that immensity was still ever-present for Enna. She looked at the various carts and tents that lined the street, then at the storefronts behind and in-between, and then still at the rooftops, her eyes landing finally on that great spire in the centre of the city. Even in so vast and dense a place, one need only turn around to see the main tower of the castle. Enna imagined, as she often did, what it must be like to be that high up, to have a view so all-encompassing. She then began to muse about the world outside of Hallowspire, about the stories she'd heard of the rest of the Kingdoms: the great arcane university of Lohvast, the great sprawling ports of Ghest where ships sailed to parts unknown to Enna, like the vast mountains and deserts of Majadrin.

She began to wonder if, perhaps, that was where the fae-folk originated from, from those far-flung places out past Majadrin, or perhaps on the other side of the ocean that bordered Lohvast's mountainous coast. Enna had never seen an elf, or a gnome, but she had heard stories growing up; fantastic tales of how the fae-folk were naturally imbued with arcane power, how they could move from here to there without moving, or charm mortal folk into following their every command. She remembered as a young girl talking with other children, some of whom were told by their parents that the fae-folk came in the night to steal away children who didn't do as their parents asked. Enna had always thought that sounded a bit silly; if elves and gnomes and other fae-folk could do all manner of fantastic things, what would they want with boring old mortal children?

As was often the case, Enna's thoughts were broken by a nearby voice. "Excuse me milady," spoke a familiar, hearty voice "I was wondering if I might trouble you for some carrots and potatoes?" Enna looked up to see a familiar, if aged face with a great black beard, bright violet eyes and a familiar, if similarly aged tricorn hat.

Enna's eyes widened and she nearly squealed in delight. "Adrik!" she gasped.

The dwarf looked at Enna, trying to understand the nature of her reaction. Finally, noticing the pendant on her neck, his memory began to jog, and he shook his thick index finger, trying to place a name. "Of course... Summerlark!"

"Yes!" she nodded excitedly "Enna Summerlark! We met on market day nearly eight years ago, you, and I, and my mother."

"Of course!" he chuckled. "By Othar's beard, has it been that long?"

"It has. I'd been hoping you'd return to Rheth on another market day. Where have you been?"

"Around the world and back, milady Older, though doubtful any wiser." he laughed. "And you, milady, my have you grown into as lovely a woman as your mother, if my mind serves me well. Living a life of adventure, or have you settled down with a fine Hallowspire farm boy?"

Enna blushed slightly. "Nothing quite so exciting," she admitted "I'm just here with my dad, selling what we grow and make, same as it's been the last four years."

"Ahh, so Master Summerlark had the sense to leave his lovely daughter to charm unsuspecting men out of their coin." Adrik winked knowingly "I knew when I met milady that she came from intelligent stock."

Enna laughed and shook her head. "Actually, he's off to look for some malachite for my mum; she wants them to hang about the house come winter. And please, Adrik, call me Enna."

"Ah, milady should have mentioned sooner! I've more Braashine malachite than I've use for. I'll offer the master a fairer price than the scam artists with which these streets are no doubt rife! Do you know whereabouts he was headed?"

Enna nodded "Of course. Hold on just a moment, I'll pack up what's here and walk with you."

"Too kind of you, milady Enna" Adrik said with a bow. "Allow me to help; we mustn't waste another moment, else your father falls victim to some fleecer.

The two packed up the display quickly, Enna locked up the wagon, and they headed down the winding streets of Rheth in search of Randis. Mundane as it was, Enna's heart was racing, as this was the closest to adventure as she assumed she would ever be.

CHAPTER NINE

R andis Summerlark perused the wagons and tents that lined the streets. As much as he teased his wife that she didn't often come out for market day because she'd spend whatever he'd made, it was in fact Randis who had a notoriously loose purse string. As a merchant, Randis often had spots in the Summerlark house that were floor-to-ceiling with strange wares and finds he'd picked up while on the road. When it came time to leave that life behind him, said finds went with it. He and Tessa had the land on their property to farm, but they had never had the want or need before Enna. Between the decision to renounce his mercantile life and the fact that there were now three bellies that needed filling, Randis liquidated every oddity and curious find he'd acquired on the road as a means of funding the transformation of all the rough, malleable land on the Summerlark property into a fully functional farmstead. Since then, there was a not-insignificant part of Randis that felt like a piece of the Summerlark home was missing, and as a result it was not uncommon for him to come home after market day with some small tchotchske that he could leave somewhere about the house. Tessa knew how much of her husband was left out on the road, and so she didn't mind, provided his little novelties were not purchased for too large a price.

Randis stopped at a booth that caught his eye: an old man selling statuettes made of whittled wood. The pieces were beautiful, clearly the old man had spent years perfecting his craft. As Randis looked along the small table, he saw various animals, fish, deer, bears, and cats. Other pieces were more practical, bowls and cups and knife hilts, but with designs carved into them that gave them a unique aesthetic. One piece caught Randis' eye in particular: a redwood statuette of a frolicking satyr, prancing on one cloven hoof, and flute to his mouth. The piece was painted, and had small semiprecious stones inlaid in certain places.

"Fantastic, aren't they?" Randis looked to his right to see a halfling admiring the works as well. "I particularly like the owl; reminds me of home."

"They're fine pieces, indeed." Randis nodded, and extended his hand "Randis Summerlark."

The halfling began to introduce himself, but paused a moment. "Ulmo Blacktrout." he said finally.

"Blacktrout, eh? Didn't know old Garret had any relatives in the area."

"Ah, well..." O'doc stumbled slightly "we're... new to the area."

"I see." Randis nodded. "Well, welcome to Hallowspire. It's usually a bit quiet, but most folks in the kingdom prefer it that way."

O'doc smiled, masking the fact that he feared his cover might be blown. Of all the people in the kingdom who could have introduced themselves, it had to be someone who knew the person whose identity the halfling was borrowing. What's more, O'doc had an innate sense that there was more to this individual than his outward appearance. The man looked enough like a simple farmer, come to market day to peddle some roots or squash, but his face belied that. There was a wisdom, O'doc sensed, a worldliness about this man. He had been places, seen things, and would probably not take long to ascertain that O'doc and Erasmus were not who they claimed to be.

Thankfully for the fretting halfling, the man's attention turned down the road, to the sound of clattering armour. O'doc turned to see the source of the commotion: four King's Guards, replete with shields and pole arms, were abruptly and intrusively searching the vendors' carts and tents. "Is that common?" O'doc asked Randis, still staring.

"No, it's not. The Guard'll walk through the streets, occasionally ask to have a peek in someone's cart, but I've been coming here on market day for years, and I never saw them like this..."

The pair watched as the scene unfolded; Guards digging through goods aggressively, occasionally taking certain items and confiscating them. The owners of the confiscated goods, some wares and some personal belongings, would then pull out their coin, handing what seemed to be a substantial amount of it to one of the Guard. The whole ordeal caused O'doc's unease to shift from Randis to the fact that the Guards were quickly encroaching on a wagon being tended to by half-elf who was, generally speaking, a less than cooperative individual. He quickly excused himself and hurried over to he and Erasmus' makeshift display.

The halfling reached the wagon just in time to hear Erasmus arguing with a Guard, a scenario that O'doc knew, given their situation, would not play out well.

"What do you mean you're 'required' to search my belongings?"

"New ordinance that came into effect: on the orders of Archmage Tyn the King's Guard are to inspect the belongings of market day vendors. Any vendors caught with items deemed arcane or fae paraphernalia will have said items confiscated by the Kingdom and be fined or jailed."

"This is absurd, this is my first time vending!"

"Well this is all just part of the regular process for you, then."

Before Erasmus could offer a retort that would undoubtedly result in the use of a pole arm, O'doc stepped in to attempt to diffuse the situation. "My good sir," he addressed the Guard "I can assure you that we are not harbouring any such restricted items. We are well aware of Hallowspire's feelings toward arcana, and would never deign to infringe upon them."

"Be that as it may," the Guard responded "orders are orders. Once your stock has been deemed legal, you may continue to operate for the remainder of the day."

It was then that the Guard rummaging through the wagon emerged with a small round case that protruded long and slender at one end. "Oi, Tharn," he called to the first Guard "What do ye make of this?"

Erasmus' eyes nearly leaped from their sockets as he rushed to try and grab it. "No no no, gentlemen, that's my mandolin. I'm a bard by trade, I need that!"

The second Guard stopped Erasmus with a large gauntlet-clad hand while the first flipped up the bronze clasps on the case, opening it to inspect the instrument. "Hmm, well the front looks plain enough." The Guard removed one gauntlet and removed the mandolin from its case, clasping its neck tightly.

"Be careful." Erasmus said with bated breath "She was given to me by my mother." it took the half-elf all the willpower in the world not to sound as if he were pleading, and whatever was left not to swing at the guards and steal back his beloved instrument.

"Hey, Tharn..." the second Guard said, pointing to the neck of the mandolin "look at these symbols on this part. Looks kind of funny to me..." The first Guard flipped the mandolin back over, looking at the designs inlaid on the fretboard.

"You're right." the first guard responded "Sir, the iconography on this item has been deemed to be of fae origin, and as such is in violation of Hallowspire law. As such, it is to be confiscated. You may either pay a fine of fifty gold crowns, or be imprisoned below Castle Rheth until next market day."

"No, you can't!" Erasmus shook angrily.

"Please, sirs," O'doc stepped in to interject "Surely there's some kind of misunderstanding. Perhaps we can reach some manner of agreement?"

The first guard continued to hold the mandolin. "Fifty crowns, or I will place you both in irons right now."

"The hells you will!" Erasmus reached for the instrument, prompting the second guard to grab him, and throw back the hood of his cloak, revealing the subtle points of his ears.

"Oi, this one's part fae-folk!" the Guard exclaimed.

The first Guard's eyes widened, then turned to O'doc. "Shackle him." he said without looking at his partner. "You... you are guilty of aiding and abetting a fae, and/or an unapproved user of arcana." the guard dropped the mandolin on the ground, grabbed the petrified halfling, and placed him in iron shackles. "You are both coming with us."

CHAPTER TEN

From the distance, Randis could hear the commotion from where the halfling headed. Much as he would have liked to see what was wrong, he turned his attention back to the statuettes. That Blacktrout fellow seemed affable enough, but if he was in some kind of trouble, Randis knew better than to get himself involved. It was callous of him, but it was necessary. He saw two individuals out of the corner of his eye being dragged away from that general area, and hoped the halfling wasn't one of them. He stepped aside as two of the King's Guard approached the old man's display. They seemed noticeably bothered, probably as a result of whoever was being dragged away. Still, there was an aggression and irritability with which the two acted that rubbed Randis the wrong way. The one snatched up the statuette of the Satyr, the one Randis had been eying, and shook it in the old man's face, shouting.

"What in the hells have you got here?! Peddlin' off some kind of half-man half-goat abomination to the good, law-abiding people of this city? You some kind of shaman or something? Pushing your weird, unnatural fae trash on impressionable minds?"

"No, I..." the old vendor stood, stunned "it's just a nick-knack, something I make to pass the time, I've sold them on market day before..."

"Well that was before." the Guard spat. "Tharn, toss this trash in the sack." he said, tossing the statuette to the other Guard before turning his attention back to the old vendor. "Now, fifty pieces or I drag you to the castle to rot for a month."

"What? But I don't carry that kind of money to market..."

"Gold or irons, old man."

"Please, just let me return tomorrow, I'll..."

Before the old man could finish, the Guard brought the back of his gauntlet-clad hand across the man's face. Randis saw blood come from the poor vendor's mouth, and heard the unmistakable crack of a broken jaw as the man flew back and slumped to the ground, unconscious.

***

Enna did not expect the commotion she saw as she turned onto the cobblestone side street with Adrik in tow. King's Guard marched past her and the dwarf, rummaging through the vendors' areas. Looking ahead, she saw her father at a small display. There was an old man, bloody and limp on one side of the display table, and on the other side, her father was shouting at one of the King's Guard. Another of the Guard had him in an arm lock. She was out of earshot, but stopped a moment, trying to make sense of what she was seeing.

"I gather that gentleman being accosted by the Guard would be milady Enna's father?" Adrik asked.

"Dad..." Enna whispered "Adrik, something's wrong, we have to help him."

"At your service, milady. What ho!" the two began a sprint toward the scene, but stopped short at the sight of Randis evidently spitting on the one Guard's face, prompting the second to swing a large armoured forearm across the back of Randis' head.

Enna's mind raced. She wanted nothing more than to scream for her father and run to him, but in that moment everything around her seemed to stop. In an instant, she saw the symbols, those unknown sounds from within the depths of her mind. She felt the small crystalline pendant around her neck begin to grow warm, as though it were acting as a focusing lens for what was becoming ever clearer in her mind's eye. All of a sudden the shapes, the representations of tone and cadence and inflection, were as clear in Enna's mind as if they had been written in parchment and placed not two feet from her eyes. The shapes guided her mouth, her tongue, and her voice. Enna Summerlark had meant to scream for her father, but instead, different words, strange words she had never heard before erupted from her.

"*A AMIN I' SUL!*"

All at once, an unseen concussive force rushed from Enna's hands. The force knocked over Randis, as well as the two King's Guard surrounding him. Adrik looked up at her, mouth agape, as the clattering sound of armour quickly escalated behind them. "By Othar's beard..." he said barely above a whisper, and with a mix of wonder and terror. "Enna, you're an arcanist?"

Enna turned to look at the dwarf. Her vision was blurry, and everything was spinning around her. What had just happened? What did she just say? She felt a deep fatigue; a kind of exhaustion that she had never felt before, even on the most laborious days on the farm. She tried to speak to Adrik, but could only muster a weak "Adrik...I..." before collapsing, the dwarf catching her limp frame.

Adrik Thornmallet had only a moment of contemplation before the King's Guard rushed up behind him, but in that moment, much about Enna Summerlark began to make sense. The name, her slight frame and stature, and looking at her, he noticed a silver ear cuff clasped over the top of one of her ears. In the instant that Adrik came to his astonished conclusion, he felt a dull, bludgeoning strike across the back of his head, and everything went black.

CHAPTER ELEVEN

Randis Summerlark awoke on a cold stone floor. His head throbbed, and he could taste blood. His vision was slightly blurry, unaided by the fact that wherever he was not particularly well lit. As his eyes came into focus he saw, sitting on a wooden bench directly across from where he lay, a familiar halfling, feet up, hand over his mouth in quiet contemplation. "You..." he groaned at the halfling "Ulmo Blacktrout, right?"

"Ah, you're awake." O'doc said, barely turning his head to acknowledge Randis. "It's Overhill, actually. O'doc Overhill."

Randis sat up, and let out a short, dire laugh. "Figures. You have any idea where we are?"

"Well, after my idiotic associate got us shackled, we were dragged into a side alley. Those pompous brutes knocked us both to our knees and put sacks over our heads. He and I weren't separated until after we were marched into a door and down some stairs, and now here we sit in a cell, so the nearest I can guess is that we're under the city somewhere."

"Fantastic." Randis rubbed the back of his head. More blood. "I don't remember too much... I got in those Guards' faces for swinging at that old man, poor bastard likely died from the hit. Got a bit rowdy and had one of 'em cuff me upside the head, then I remember hearing this voice: sounded like my daughter, but said something I didn't understand. Then black, and now here I am..."

"Your daughter, eh? Interesting..."

"Why? What's so interesting about it?" Randis said hotly. "You know something I don't?"

"I know what I heard in the distance," O'doc offered "just before they put that sack on my head. Seemed an odd thing to hear in Rheth, of all places."

"Well, what was it?" Randis demanded "What was that voice?"

"What I heard, and what I can assume you heard, was an arcane spell." O'doc explained "Specifically an elemental conjuration spell: wind if I'm not mistaken. A fancy party trick, but not the most utilitarian spell. All the same, not at all expected in the streets of Rheth..." As informed and eloquent as his response was, it was clear the halfling's mind was primarily focused on other things.

"Well, if it's just a 'party trick', then why is it the last thing I heard before winding up here? And how could Enna have known how to do that?" The questions were asked as much to O'doc as they were to Randis himself.

"Maybe your friend there could tell you more when he comes to." O'doc motioned to the unconscious dwarf about five feet away from where Randis sat. "You and he were thrown in here at the same time; Guards were muttering something about a 'great arcane attack'. I assume you were in the same general area when all this happened."

Randis looked over at the dwarf, then crawled across the floor and proceeded to shake him. "Hey, you! Dwarf, wake up!" he whispered hoarsely.

The dwarf groaned and began to stir. "By all the great thanes, where the blazes am I?"

"Were you there, in the street? Did you see a girl? What happened?" Randis was practically throttling the dwarf in a bout of paternal concern.

"Hold a moment, friend." the dwarf said, putting a hand on Randis' arm to cease the unwanted motion. "First, introductions: you are Master Randis Summerlark, no?"

"How do you know who I am?" Randis pulled him close. "Where's Enna?"

"Be calm!" the dwarf said, pulling Randis' hand from his shirt. "I am Adrik Thornmallet. I was accompanying your daughter, as she told me you were in need of malachite, of which I had an abundance."

This seemed to quell Randis' mounting frustrations, as he at least recognized the dwarf's name from Enna's tales. He stood up, offering a hand to help Adrik to his feet. "So you were with Enna, what happened?"

Adrik dusted himself off, picked his hat up off the ground, and dusted it off before placing it back on his head. "The young lady and I came upon you in the midst of an altercation, and had planned on rushing to your assistance, when she let loose that arcane spell. I caught the poor lass just in time to be knocked out myself."

"I'm sorry," Randis rubbed his temples as they throbbed "did you say Enna cast that spell?"

"Indeed she did. Quite the spectacle, if ever I had seen one." Adrik took notice of the side and back of Randis' head. "You're bleeding, seems fresh. May I?"

"It's nothing." Randis dismissed "How could Enna have cast that spell?"

"It was my hope that you might be able to inform me of that." Adrik responded, grabbing a nearby stool and positioning himself behind Randis so as to see the wounds better. "Be honest, the young lady herself looked entirely surprised by what she had done." He looked closely at the back of Randis' head "This is worse than you think. Please, sit."

Randis begrudgingly obliged the dwarf, sitting on the stool and allowing him to prod at the wounds. "We need to staunch the bleeding; it will not fix the problem completely, but I doubt they'll allow us a needle and some gut in our current accommodations. You there," he called to O'doc, who was still staring contemplatively, "have you been awake long? What have we got at our disposal presently?"

O'doc, his mind elsewhere, looked over at the dwarf. "Not a terrible lot, seeing as they took just about all my belongings, and I assume yours as well. Why not just use a piece of a shirt?"

"The larger cut is too deep." Adrik explained. "It requires medical attention, it needs...." his violet eyes darted around the room, his dwarven heritage allowing him a greater view in the dim light than either the human or halfling could hope for. "Ahh, there's just the thing!" he exclaimed as he darted over to one corner of the cell, and began hopping and swatting at the upper corner with his hat.

"Did he hit *his* head?" O'doc asked, looking confusedly at the hopping dwarf.

"If my head's as bad as he says, I certainly hope not."

After a few moments, Adrik looked at his hat and, seeming satisfied, hurried back to his patient. "Couldn't have asked for better supplies," the dwarf mused half to himself "given the present situation."

"What do you mean?" Randis said, suddenly much more tentative towards Adrik's aid. "What were you doing in that corner?"

"Gathering cobwebs, of course."

O'doc looked over, "Cobwebs? Are you actually mad, or are you planning on using some kind of strange dwarven magic?"

"Neither, thank you very much sir!" Adrik replied, taken aback by the comment. "I'll have you know that my sister's husband is chief cleric to Thane Harbek himself! It would behoove me as an intellectual not to have learned a few tricks of his trade." Adrik took the cobwebs from his hat and bundled them up until they nearly resembled a kind of dry paste. He then applied them to Randis' larger wound, spreading the web evenly across the deep gash. "There." he said with finality "It's far and away from a proper stitching job, but it ought to be enough to take care of that until we manage to get out of this cell."

"Thank you." Randis said, nearly touching the makeshift dressing, but stopping himself after remembering what it was. "How long until you figure we do get out of here?"

A smirk played across O'doc's face, as his gaze remained fixated on the locked cell door. "With the right timing and a fair bit of luck," he said "sooner than either of you might expect."

CHAPTER TWELVE

Erasmus Stonehand sat in a plain stone cell. After he and O'doc had been taken away in shackles, blindfolded and separated, he remembered being taken through a door, going through a number of twisting corridors, and both ascending and descending a number of sets of stairs. Erasmus was no stranger to jails; one does not become an expert smuggler overnight, and along the way he had made some missteps. He was aware of the fact that in cities such as Rheth, where the streets were entirely devoid of any questionable action, and where guards could be seen at every corner, the jails were typically both substantial, and in a state of constant occupation. This was why Erasmus sat uneasy in his cell; there was an unsettling lack of sound around him. He was unaware of how long this particular corridor of cells stretched, but he had expected some kind of bustle, drunks mumbling, deadbeats pleading, and killers threatening. Instead, there was nothing. Not even the sound or sight of guards, past the one who placed him in his cell, and one shortly after who placed a young woman in the cell directly across from him.

The woman was unconscious when she was brought. The guard had lain her on the cot in her cell, where she came to about an hour later. She seemed confused and distraught, shaking at the bars of the cell, banging and calling for someone to help. Soon after, it seemed as though she realized the futility of what she was doing, and she sat, clearly desperate, and began to cry. Erasmus hadn't made an effort to engage in any kind of conversation with the girl initially. Instead, he thought it best to observe, as perhaps there were some reason that the two of them were the only ones in this corridor. Everything about the woman seemed to discount this theory; Erasmus was a seasoned smuggler, and a man of the road. He was told that he was being jailed for being of fae heritage. This woman, dressed in her farm clothes, looked like she was plucked straight from her chicken coop and tossed in that cell. Her accent as she cried for help made it indicative of the fact that she was native of Hallowspire. Her clear despair was a sign that this entire experience was new. What possible reason could there be for Erasmus to be the only other person there besides this local country bumpkin?

Gradually, the woman regained her composure. She sat, thinking for several minutes. Erasmus watched intently as she then stood up to face the cell door, widened her stance, and placed her hands out in front of her. He listened as she spoke, his interest heightened by what he heard.

"'A....'a amin I' sul!"

Nothing happened, but things now began to make sense: the woman was an arcanist! Erasmus had thought he had heard that spell called out before he was dragged through that door back out on the streets of Rheth, and this woman was likely the source. It would have been an impressive feat indeed for an arcanist to have been training and studying for years right under the noses of Hallowspire's higher powers. He heard her try the spell again, and again nothing happened. There was an uncertainty in the way she called out the incantation; perhaps she was still relatively inexperienced. A third time, Erasmus heard the woman call out the spell, and a third time nothing happened. He knew it wouldn't work, and he knew why. "You're wasting your time." he called to her.

The sudden interjection of another voice amid the silence caused the woman to startle. She looked across to Erasmus' cell, clearly frustrated. "And how would you know that?"

"I admire the fact that you're trying to cast," he replied "but you know as well as I that trying that without your implement is an exercise in futility."

"What do you mean," the woman left her stance and walked toward the cell door "my implement?"

Erasmus' eyebrows raised in disbelief. "What do I.... are you serious? Do you actually expect me to believe that you're an arcanist, and you have no idea what your implement is?"

"I'm not an arcanist." she said defensively "Why do people keep saying that?"

"Well, the attempted spellcasting might account for that. If you're not an arcanist, then how and where did you learn the incantation you keep trying?"

"I..." the woman paused, as if trying to uncloud her memory. "I don't know... I just saw my father being arrested. I wanted to help, and then..." she stopped, and looked at Erasmus. "Wait, why am I telling you this, who are you anyway?"

"Erasmus Stonehand," he said with a bow "worldly and world class bard, at your service. And you?"

"Enna." the woman said, looking carefully at Erasmus "Enna Summerlark. Are you an elf?"

"Only on my father's side," Erasmus answered reservedly. "The other half of me is just as human as you."

"Is that how you know about arcana?"

"Not exactly," he said "but to its credit, I'm told it helps."

"So you're an arcanist?"

"Hardly." he responded "I'm a performer, first and foremost, and let's just say that along the way I discovered that I can use my craft to *augment* my audience's opinions."

"So you use arcana to make people think you're a better bard?" Enna asked with an apparent distaste.

"Hey, don't judge me!" Erasmus countered "It's a matter of business; any fool with two working hands can learn three chords and make some coin playing for drunks. I create art, and I don't think it's unfair to ask for a bit greater remuneration for that. Occasionally, my audiences need some convincing."

"That's low."

Erasmus shrugged "It's a living. We can't all live on lush farmsteads."

"How did you know I lived on a farm?"

"I'm observant. Now, about your supposed lack of an implement..." Erasmus was cut off by the distant sound of a door, followed by footsteps. He motioned to Enna to remain quiet, and she needed no further prompting.

Walking down the hall was a hooded individual in a long, plain brown robe. The footfalls were quiet, juxtaposed by the faint clinking of a keyring. The figure stopped between the two cells, and pulled back the hood to reveal an elven male. Though he had a youthful face, and his hair was a rich chestnut colour, there was an agedness in his golden eyes, and he spoke with a voice that sounded worn by the years. "The two of you will be accompanying me."

Chapter Thirteen

In a small, nondescript room, a figure in an opulent azure and gold robe was in the midst of a conversation with another similarly robed figure, in a similarly nondescript room, hundreds of miles away. Their voices were as one, each speaking in a low, droning monotone that was virtually indistinguishable from the other.

"The were-rat has been dealt with," said the one "his loyalty is now strictly aligned with the Mission."

"Good." the other answered "his mercurial nature was becoming problematic."

"An unnecessary liability." The first agreed "One must hope the were-rat's agents are more obedient."

"Indeed, this remains to be seen. One cannot stress the speed with which time is dwindling. Failure will result in a need for a more obvious presence, which is not ideal."

"Agreed. Subtlety is a key factor in the execution of the Mission. The subject must remain complacent."

"Else the Mission is failed."

The two robed figures then raised their arms, and spoke in unison, in a low chant:

"So has it been said,"
"So has it been heard,"
"So has it been understood,"
"So shall it be done."

At the end of the chant, the simulacrum in either room faded, leaving only the individual figures, each in their identical rooms, hundreds of miles apart. One of the figures stepped out of the room, and into a large bedchamber. It was then that Derrus Tyn, Archmage of Hallowspire, removed his azure and gold robe, placing it on a hook, and closing the door to the small room, leaving the appearance of a large bookshelf in its place. He took his crimson Archmage's robe off another hook next to the bookcase and put it on, doing his best to smooth any wrinkles or creases in it.

The Archmage looked about his bedchamber. A large canopy bed sat along the middle of the far wall, replete with sheets of the finest silk in the Four Kingdoms. Bookshelves filled with histories, memoires, tomes, and of course arcane grimoires lined most of the area of the other walls, with space enough left in one section for a door into a large closet, which Tyn, having little need for an extensive wardrobe, had converted into a personal study. He had done well for himself in garnering this position, and he was more than content to do everything within his power to retain it. The Archmage looked about the bedchamber contentedly one last time, straightened his robes, and exited out to speak with the King.

***

Archmage Tyn entered the large throne room of Castle Rheth, walking along a plush red velvet past row on row of marble columns, royal family portraits, and little else. The King had long since removed the old statues and bas reliefs, most depicting fae imagery and other things he had deemed to be in poor taste. As such, the walls of the throne room were nearly bare, giving the expansive chamber an incredibly stark and foreboding feel. King Renton sat at the other end of the throne room, on a large, plush throne. The King did not sit in the throne often, and more often than not preferred not to be in the throne room unless at court. Barring that, King Renton only ever sat in the throne room if he were worried or upset, a fact that Archmage Tyn knew well, and as such walked into the room pensively. Tyn had an idea of what drew the King to the throne room on this day, and was hoping that the explanation he was prepared to offer would be enough to satisfy the King in regards to so important a subject.

"Your Grace," the Archmage bowed low as he approached the throne "you bid an audience with me?"

"Archmage Tyn," the King began, speaking slowly and holding the bridge of his nose in frustration, "Please explain to me why there are whispers in the street of some rogue arcanist running amok through the market?"

Indeed, the Archmage had heard the report of the girl who conjured up a wind powerful enough to knock down two of the Guard, as well as some ruffian they were arresting. Still, though, this was information the King could do without. "I have spoken with a number of the Guard on patrol today, your Grace, and I have heard nothing of the sort."

"Well the streets are abuzz with it!" the King boomed "Tell me, how do you explain that?"

"Extrapolation, your grace." the Archmage stated plainly. "Indeed, there was some ruffian activity in the streets today, but it was dealt with quickly. Perhaps the combination of that and the sudden implementation of your ordinance regarding the seizure of arcane paraphernalia today led to miscommunication among the people of Rheth."

The king pursed his lips, and began to look through the Archmage thoughtfully. "You say there was 'ruffian activity' today?"

"Yes, your grace, a handful of belligerent merchants, evidently in violation of the new ordinance. They were dealt with swiftly and with little commotion. I assure you, your Grace, nothing happened on the streets today that has not been dealt with in the past, nor will any of this linger in the minds of your people for more than a few days, at worst."

"Perhaps" the King began to muse, as much to himself as to the Archmage, "enforcing this latest ordinance so hurriedly was a misstep. The people are clearly reacting to it negatively..."

"No, your Grace," Tyn said reassuringly, approaching the throne "the people will understand in time. If nothing else, today's incident will simply act as a helpful reminder of the importance of following Hallowspire law to the letter." Tyn took his hands and placed them on the King's shoulders. "Your Grace, in three decades, have I ever offered you ill advice?"

The King looked at his Archmage. The whole ordeal did not sit well in his mind, and yet all he had heard was whispered hearsay and speculation. As such, he trusted Tyn enough not to press the rumours further, putting them out of his mind, at least for the time being. He sighed heavily, albeit with minimal relief as a result. "So what of the belligerent merchants?" he asked.

"Gone before the night's end, banned from Rheth for one month; merciful, but stern enough to send a message." Archmage Tyn bowed as he king nodded his approval "And fear not, my best men are handling it."

CHAPTER FOURTEEN

Enna and Erasmus walked down a long narrow corridor, being followed and guided by the elf, who had since pulled his hood back over his head. The three had spent the last hour twisting and turning though a complex series of hallways, many having no features with which to distinguish one hallway from the next. The two prisoners were shackled together by wrist irons, each cuff emblazoned with some manner of strange and intricate markings that neither could understand, nor even recognize. After an hour of nothing but the sounds of footsteps, Enna finally spoke.

"You aren't one of the King's Guard, are you?"

"No." the elf answered "I serve the kingdom through different avenues."

"An elf serving the Great Bastion of Humanity?" Erasmus asked with more than a hint of incredulity "Care to elaborate as to how that even makes sense?"

"It is true," the elf responded "there are no fae beings to be found in Hallowspire. Some do manage to come and go, on rare occasions, but few" he accentuated pointedly "are careless or stupid enough to be found."

"Hey, now see here," Erasmus defended "If it weren't for those thugs you people try to pass off as law enforcement trying..."

"To take your mandolin; your arcane implement, no doubt." the elf finished "I am aware of why you both were brought here, that is why I came to you."

"What's going to happen to us?" Enna asked. The elf was aloof in his speech, and because of that Enna was not sure she wanted to hear his answer.

"You needn't fear for your lives." the elf responded "You have my word that I intend no harm upon either of you, but know that you will both be under my supervision, and will see only myself and each other."

"Do we have a choice in the matter?" Erasmus asked sarcastically.

"You do. In the last thirty years, there have been five individuals other than yourselves imprisoned for being of fae origin and/or the unapproved use of arcana. Three stayed in my care, eventually to be approved for release by Archmage Tyn." the elf said stoically. "The other two were deemed unworkable and were executed."

Enna felt a weight in the pit of her stomach, and gulped back a lump in her throat. "How do we know we can trust you?"

"You do not know for certain. Know, however, that I went to great lengths to secure the two of you. Had I no interest in your well-being, I could simply have left you to rot or hang."

"Well I don't trust you." Erasmus said casually.

"That is your prerogative. Know that the gallows are ever-ready for you, though I would prefer you not take that avenue."

"Believe me, I prefer this avenue here just fine." Erasmus answered defensively "Although, in all fairness, knowing your name would probably help your case slightly."

"You may call me Varis." the elf responded flatly.

"Well Varis," Erasmus continued "How do *you* know that you can trust *us*? We are all-powerful arcanists, after all." The bard didn't expect the elf would fall for the bluff, but he hoped that in challenging this "Varis" to some verbal sparring he could frustrate the elf, and possibly cause him to reveal some useful information. He was sorely disappointed when Varis' response carried the same calm as the rest of the conversation.

"For one thing, I can sense that neither of you have the skill or discipline to cast spells without your arcane implements. For another, I can assure you that far stronger arcanists than yourselves have challenged me and fell. Finally, and independent of the first two points, your shackles will not allow you to cast."

Enna looked down at the shackles, at the strange symbols and patters. In them was that strange intrinsic familiarity she felt when she saw the symbols in her mind, the ones that brought forth the intense rush of energy and force back in the street. She could not make out what the symbols on the shackles were, however, as even in their familiarity they seemed wholly foreign. "How..." she began to ask, before being shushed by Varis as they turned a corner to come to a large wooden door.

"All in its given time." the elf said. "For now, we are entering the Common cell blocks. Most in here are riff-raff, including many of the Guard, and as such the less attention we draw to ourselves the better."

Varis opened the door, on the other side of which was another long unremarkable stone corridor, at the end of which was a door identical to the one Varis had just opened. There was a change in atmosphere, however, as the trio walked down the corridor toward the far door. The air, in particular, was markedly changed, going from the stale mildew scent of prolonged periods of disuse, to the complete assault of the olfactory. Whatever lay beyond that unopened door smelled of overuse and uncleanliness; a wretched cornucopia of scents largely made up of various unsavoury human waste products. It was the kind of scent that Erasmus was expecting while in his initial cell, a scent that reminded him of past mistakes made, and one which he, and Enna would have been more than happy to do without.

Entering the Common cell blocks, the three were greeted with a sight equally as pitiful as the smell that preceded it. Row on row of dimly lit cells with barred iron doors, filled sometimes as many as six deep with various types of occupants. Vagabonds, destitute beggars, drunks both inebriated and recovering; all manner of decidedly unsightly character lined the ensuing corridors. Certain wings contained little noise, while others were deafeningly uproarious. Occasionally, prisoners would call out to the trio, slinging vulgar epithets at Erasmus and even more vulgar insinuations at Enna, often resulting in one of the patrolling King's Guard smacking the bars with a cudgel, silencing the inmates temporarily.

Enna and Erasmus kept stone-faced, their eyes ever forward, he out of restraint and she out of fear and unease. It was not until they reached a point where two hallways intersected, that Enna broke her facade. This was caused by the sight of a King's Guard marching a shackled Randis Summerlark down the hall perpendicular to the one she occupied.

"Dad?" she cried out, her voice quivering.

Randis looked to his left in disbelief. "Enna?!"

"Dad!" she ran toward her father, causing Erasmus to stumble in a forced follow, and causing Varis to attempt to seize the two. Randis, too, ran toward his daughter, getting only a few feet before his shackles, chained to his escort, ran out of slack and stopped him.

Randis began to yell at the robed individual holding his daughter at bay. "Let the girl go, she's done nothing wrong! Enna, sweet, don't worry, I'll get you out of this!"

Varis looked at the Guard. "Where are you taking this man?"

"What business is that of yours?" the Guard spat "He's just a man, not one of your fae playthings."

Varis closed in on the Guard and stared into his eyes with a burning intensity, causing the armoured and armed man to shrink into himself. "I will not repeat myself." he said with as much calm in his voice as he had shown for the past hour.

"Back... back out." the Guard stumbled over his words, unable to meet the elf's eyes. "He was just in for causing a scene; Archmage Tyn says he's free to go."

"I request a word with him before you go any further."

"Of... of course..."

Varis turned to Randis, and spoke quietly to him, the flare gone from his golden eyes. "You are the girl's father?"

"I am, and I swear to every God from here to the Fires if you've done anything..."

"She is safe, and will remain so while in my care."

Randis looked to his daughter, tears rolling down both their cheeks. "Dad, you don't need to worry. I... I trust him."

"Enna, I'll think of something, I promise."

"You have my word" Varis spoke to Randis "that no harm will befall her. On my honour, you shall receive notice to this fact often." Varis then leaned in close, whispering into Randis' ear "You have done a remarkable job in keeping the girl's secret safe. Rest assured that I will take every precaution to do the same."

Randis looked at the elf, a mixture of fear and rage in his eyes "If anything happens..."

"On the word of Varis the Silver-frond," the elf responded "if

~ 61 ~

anything is to happen to her, my life is yours to take."

Varis stepped back, allowing Enna and Randis a moment. Randis looked at his daughter with pleading eyes. "Tell mum that I'm alright," Enna choked back tears "and that I love you both, and I promise I'll see you both soon."

"Enna, I..." Randis did everything in his power to maintain his composure, to make sure that he, as always, was strong for his girl. "We'll figure something out..." he kissed his daughter on the forehead, and the Guard began to drag him away.

"You have all my love, sweet!" he called back to her as he was pulled "Be good, I'll have you home soon!"

From there, Varis led Erasmus and Enna further into the winding complex. Erasmus remained stone-faced, though now as he did so, he grabbed Enna's hand, holding it as they walked. The girl had just lost her father, and by the sound of things, everything she had ever known. She needed to know that she had someone on her side in this ordeal. Enna took the bard's hand willingly, and held it tight, but it offered little comfort, and the silence that would otherwise have filled the remainder of the walk was peppered with the soft sobbing of a girl whose entire world had been ripped away.

CHAPTER FIFTEEN

everal days passed in which Enna Summerlark did not speak. She and Erasmus were taken by the elf Varis to an area unlike the rest of the dank catacombs they had seen up to this point. Their accommodations, while not luxurious by any means, were clean and dry, with partitioned sleeping areas for both of them, replete with wash basins. There was a simple wood table in the centre section, with three plain wooden chairs. Every morning, Varis would enter, carrying a breakfast of fruits breads and cheese, as well as fresh hot water. The elf would sit at the wood table and eat with Enna and Erasmus, staying in the room with them for several hours, leaving briefly only to return with a supper usually consisting of a root stew and more bread. After supper, Varis would remain a little while longer, before leaving for the night, locking the door behind him.

Once, on the third day, Enna had spoken to Erasmus briefly after Varis had left. Erasmus had tried to spend the better part of the day prior trying to get Enna to speak, but to no avail.

"You're going to have to say something eventually." he frustratedly tried to goad her while dipping bread into his stew "At some point, you will need something, and have to tell one of us."

"Due time." Varis told Erasmus as he looked into his own stew. "The girl will speak when she is prepared to." Though Erasmus did not fully trust the elf, he heeded his advice, and made no effort to force conversation with Enna on that third day. Finally, as Erasmus began to walk toward his partitioned quarters, he heard Enna's voice from behind him.

"Why did you take my hand the other day?"

Erasmus turned around to look at the girl. "Because loneliness and helplessness can crush a person. Loneliness on its own is bad enough; it can make you feel inches tall and surrounded by giants, but a resourceful person can live with loneliness. Helplessness, on the other hand, will slowly suffocate you inside, hollow you out until you're a shell. That kind of void can be remedied, filled, but not without the help of others. If a person is lonely and helpless, then they become a prisoner, locked away and bound in their own mind and either unwilling or unable to allow others to try their hand at finding the key. I saw that in you, that wretched combination, and I wanted you to know that you weren't alone."

Enna was silent a moment allowing a small smile to form on her face as she looked at the half-elf, trying not to allow tears to form in the corners of her eyes. "And here I thought you were going to tell me you were planning on seducing me." she said incredulously.

"Please," Erasmus laughed "you're not my type, you're far too young, and what kind of man would I be to take advantage of a distraught prisoner girl?"

"Exactly the kind of man I thought you were." Enna retorted "Not now, though. You're a good person, Erasmus Stonehand, thank you for that."

"Don't go telling people," Erasmus smirked "I do have a reputation to uphold." He then turned back around to walk to his quarters, and Enna did the same, finding that sleep was able to come to her much easier than it had in the last two days.

***

The next day, Enna felt entirely different than she had the days prior. She still spent her breakfast in silence, but not because of the despair she felt before. Rather, she was curious, specifically about Varis, who though he was nearly ever-present, was still very much shrouded in mystery. Enna looked at him while she ate, trying her hardest to be discreet in her staring, all the while racking questions in her head that she wanted answered about the elf. All the while, though she wanted these questions answered, she was intimidated by his presence. Nothing about Varis was outwardly threatening, and yet she felt there was something underlying that would cause anyone with common sense to tread lightly when attempting to learn anything about him. One thing that particularly caught Enna's attention, was what appeared to be a tattoo on the inside of the elf's left wrist; a symbol that reminded her of the shackles he had put on her and Erasmus. Without realizing, her eyes lingered on the tattoo long enough for Varis to notice, and subtly tug the sleeve of his robes down over his wrist.

"It is an elven glyph." Varis said plainly as Enna looked away. "Is there anything else you would like to know? You need only ask."

"Well, quite a lot, really," Enna admitted "but I wouldn't want to pry..."

"There's no need to worry yourself." Varis responded "Ask what you wish. If I choose not to answer, then I will not. If you choose to press the issue, then you will be prying."

Enna began to think, trying to come up with a question that didn't seem too personal or offensive. In that moment, Erasmus spoke up. "Something I'd like to know Varis," he reached for an apple, and took a large bite, continuing as he chewed "What is this Kingdom's problem, anyway? Why the anti-fae, anti-arcane sentiments? I don't recall ever reading anything about any great catastrophe that befell the place at the hands of an army of elven arcanists."

"You would not have been old enough to know what happened." Varis said "Though, even if you had, and even if you had been in Hallowspire at the time, you would not have heard the truth. You see, roughly thirty years ago, Hallowspire was an open, prosperous Kingdom, if the smallest of the Four. It was ruled by King Johannus Isevahr and his wife, Queen Selene. The two had one son, Prince Renton, who was just barely twelve when it happened."

"When what happened?" Enna interjected.

Varis turned to Enna and continued. "The King and Queen died suddenly, and mysteriously. Hallowspire's Archmage at the time had told the people that it was a freak accident that the two were on their way to Ghest for a trade meeting when a bolt of lightning struck their coach whilst on the road one night. In fact, it was the Archmage who found the bodies, here in Castle Rheth, lying next to one another in one of the rooms at the highest point of the great central spire. An incredibly secret investigation went underway for several months to determine what had happened. The top court physicians were only able to glean what were *not* the causes of death: no manner of disease, no poison, it left them baffled. The Archmage himself suspected some manner of arcana, but could not think of any arcane spell known to men that could have taken the King and Queen's lives so instantaneously, and with so little evidence of the fact.

"Suffice it to say, young Prince Renton was nothing if not distraught. The Archmage tried to console and counsel the young Prince, as was his duty as acting Regent, yet his efforts proved largely fruitless; there was a resentment present in the Prince, one borne of a young man who had, all of the sudden, lost his parents, only to have them hurriedly replaced by someone whom he knew largely by title alone. All of the sudden, rumours began to surface about the Castle. You see, King Johannus had plans to have the Prince taught arcana, in the hopes that when he did ascend the throne as king that Renton would be well-equipped to handle a world in which the use of arcana was becoming more prominent. As such, the King enlisted a man named Derrus Tyn, one of the finest minds at the Arcane University in Lohvast, to teach Prince Renton all he could. The rumors circulated quickly, stating that the King and Queen's deaths were in fact an assassination, one carried out by a fearful Archmage, worried that the continuation of Prince Renton's arcane education would allow him to eventually take on the role of both King and Archmage, resulting in the abolition of the position and title of Archmage in Hallowspire. The Archmage was taken from his chambers in the dead of night and thrown in the prison under Castle Rheth, the young King Renton appointing Tyn as new Archmage of Hallowspire.

"From there, much of the laws and ordinances that make Hallowspire what it is today were swiftly implemented. The King, I suspect greatly under the influence of Tyn, decreed that all use of arcana within the Kingdom was illegal unless it was given prior explicit approval by the Archmage, citing that arcana was too powerful and dangerous a force to be unregulated. Shortly thereafter, it was decreed that any beings of fae origin, including those half-blooded, were no longer welcome in the kingdom, as their historically-proven aptitude for arcana made them unnecessary liabilities to the safety of the Kingdom." Varis took the last piece of cheese from the plate. "And so, here we are today."

"So what makes you so special that you're exempt from this fae ban?" Erasmus asked.

"Make no mistake Erasmus, as I said when we met, I am a prisoner as are you both. However, I possess abilities that Archmage Tyn sees as assets, and as such, I am afforded certain privileges as a result."

"You were the Archmage to King Johannus, weren't you?" Enna asked.

Varis said nothing, gathering the empty breakfast platters and piling them on the corner of the wooden table. He looked to Enna. "Well, now that you've decided to warm to me, I think it's time I began both of your instruction."

CHAPTER SIXTEEN

Six days came and went since O'doc Overhill and Adrik Thornmallet met in a cell somewhere beneath the city of Rheth. The lack of light made it impossible to measure time, save for the food given to the two cellmates twice daily by a Guard on duty. In that time, O'doc had barely moved from the position in which Adrik and discovered him when he was awoken by Randis Summerlark those six days earlier. Repositioning himself only to eat and sleep, and even then only doing so slightly, O'doc remained on the wooden bench nearest the cell door, legs up, and eyes gazing outward contemplatively.

In those six days, the pair learned a great deal about one another. Adrik had learned that O'doc came from a long line of halfling arcanists and, while he was well educated, forsook his lineage to find his own fortune, albeit for reasons he chose not to discuss. O'doc had learned that Adrik's greatest passion was for alchemy, and that his mercantile lifestyle was largely utilitarian, serving as both a means to fund his passion, as well as a means of finding new substances across the Kingdoms. Indeed, in those six days the two developed a camaraderie that, although stemming from indefinite incarceration, was genuine. And yet, amid all that, O'doc stayed resolute in his contemplation, and Adrik had not yet asked why. Finally, after six days had come and gone, the dwarf's curiosity piqued.

"Tell me, good sir," he began, striding up to the halfling "I can assume, based on the resoluteness of your vigil, that you are either contemplating the great mysteries of life, or that you are hatching some manner of ingenious plan that, I should hope, would benefit the both of us. As such, allow me to offer this: if the former, I am sure that the insight of another well-read mind would only assist you in your quandary. If the latter, then perhaps voicing said plan aloud would enable you to better visualize it. What say you?"

"I say I think it's positively ridiculous that it took you this long to ask what in the hells I've been doing for nearly a week." O'doc smirked.

"I wished to leave you to your thoughts, offering my assistance only if prompted." Adrik explained "Yet here I stand now, nearly one week later, my curiosity having got the better of me. So, yes, I ask you, Master Overhill, by Othar's beard what in the blazes are you staring at?"

"Well," O'doc began, "since you asked so politely, I'll indulge you. Look at the lock on this door: every lock has a uniquely shaped mechanism inside that lines up with a key crafted uniquely to fit it. Over the last six days, I have been observing every passing guard, notably the ones who have brought us meals, analyzing their keys and trying to discern the shape of the one for our lock."

"So you mean to pick the lock on the cell?"

"Not just that, Adrik. Simply picking the lock on a prison cell would be a rookie mistake. No, I've also been analyzing the guards; their patrol patterns, who is scheduled when, and the like. With any luck, I could time the ideal moment for us to spring from this cell, and give us, ideally, about twenty minutes before someone discovers that the cell is empty."

"I see." Adrik said, evidently impressed. "Now, provided I don't sound like a simpleton for asking: with what were you planning to pick the lock?"

"The heel of my boot."

"The heel of your boot?"

"Exactly." O'doc looked rather pleased with himself "It's partially hollow, that's where I keep my pick. No one ever examines the heel of the boot."

"Well done, good sir!" Adrik patted O'doc on the back and chuckled. "Now, provided all goes according to plan, when exactly would be the opportune moment for this to occur?"

O'doc did the calculations in his mind. "Well, it seems the Guards down here have a three one, one off shift schedule... considering also the possibility that they may alternate where they keep watch... our best bet would likely be in another four days."

"Four days?"

O'doc nodded. "It seems long, but there are so many intricacies in the plan that a single misstep would throw the whole thing off. My father always told us 'patience breeds perfection.'"

"I see, seems a fair rule to live by." Adrik nodded thoughtfully. Shortly thereafter they heard the clinking metallic sound of one of the Guard, come to bring food to the prisoners. The guard appeared to be one who had not yet patrolled this section, at least not in the last six days. As the Guard approached O'doc and Adrik's cell, Adrik fell to the ground, clutching his stomach and making deep, agonizing moaning noises.

O'doc turned his head to look at the dwarf as the Guard reached the cell. "What's the matter with that one?" the guard asked "Is he drunk?"

"No." O'doc replied, genuinely confused "We've been in here nearly a week; he was fine not five minutes ago..."

"Well, go see what his problem is!" the Guard barked.

O'doc got up from his perch and walked hurriedly over to the writhing, grimacing dwarf, who was clutching his stomach in agony. "Adrik," he said, leaning over his companion "is everything alright?"

Adrik stared at O'doc with watering violet eyes. "Water..." he choked "I need water!"

"Alright, I'll go to the guard and..."

Before O'doc could finish, he felt Adrik's burly hands upon the collar of his shirt. The dwarf pulled O'doc in close, so close that the halfling felt the hot stale breath of a dwarf who was six days without a bath. Adrik's eyes were nearly popping out of his head as he began to throttle O'doc. "Need...water...now!" he gasped.

The Guard, witnessing the commotion, opened the cell door and marched in. "You, dwarf!" he shouted "unhand that one, or I'll have you shackled to the wall!" The Guard marched over and began trying to pry O'doc from Adrik's vice-like grasp. "I said let the halfling go!"

In an instant, Adrik released his grip on O'doc, grabbed the Guard by the back of the head, and pulled himself up. With a loud *THUNK*, Adrik's forehead met the Guard's in a violent head-butt. The Guard slumped over, unconscious, with a loud clang. Adrik rolled over, got up, and dusted himself off, while O'doc sat, stunned by the sight.

"Master O'doc," Adrik said as he adjusted his tricorn hat

"would you be so good as to procure this gentleman's keys? It would be unbecoming if he were to awaken and have an avenue of escape." O'doc got up and took the Guard's keys as Adrik ripped a piece of fabric from the sleeve of his shirt to make a makeshift gag. The two then dragged the unconscious body to the wall shackles at the far side of the cell, and proceeded to lock the Guard into them. When all was said and done, they walked out the open cell door, closed and locked it, and started off in the direction from which the guards always came down the corridor.

"Please understand, good sir, that I meant no sleight to your immeasurably well-calculated plan." Adrik said to O'doc as they walked "it is simply that my father had his own adage he imparted onto me as a boy."

"And what adage was that?"

"You can study a mine all you like, but when you see a glimmer, you best swing that pickaxe."

Chapter Seventeen

Lannister Ravenclaw sat in his bedchamber in the River Rats' guildhall in Delverbrook. The moon had long since peaked in the sky, and yet there the halfling sat, on edge, unable to sleep. It had been this way every night since his meeting with his benefactor at that accursed place a week prior. Initially, Lannister thought it to be simply unease; strange things had happened that day, and so it was only natural that he would spend a day or two slightly shaken up about the whole ordeal. As the days passed, however, Lannister's day-to-day operations became more and more difficult for him. Out on the streets, he could have sworn that he would occasionally catch a passerby staring with the intense, knowing stare of all those eyes within that nondescript building. Worse still were the voices, strange mumbled chatter during the day, and at night, some manner of ethereal chanting, a liturgical call-and-response that lasted through the night, growing louder, it seemed, with each passing day.

Escalating, as well, with each passing day, was the dull ache in Lannister's shoulder. The brand that had emerged, that strange symbol on the doors of that place where Lannister deigned not to return, had disappeared from his flesh when he reexamined it. At first, he thought it to be some kind of arcane illusion, like the simulacrum to whom he spoke; a scare tactic to keep the halfling on track with "the Mission." The dull pangs in Lannister's shoulder, reaching all the way down to his bone, disproved that. The pain added to Lannister's inability to sleep at night, as no matter how he positioned himself, he was never afforded any reprieve from the ache.

And so, there the halfling sat, bolt upright, clutching his aching shoulder; an insomnious shell of who he was. He was unable to effectively operate his guild now, and had temporarily put his second-in-command in charge of the day-to-day operations. Though Lannister had made it clear to his guild members that this was temporary, and threatened to twist a hot dagger into the backs of anyone who spoke otherwise, he knew his current state was sowing seeds of dissent amid the guild; whispers that the Guildmaster had gone mad, that his lust for power caused him to bite off more than he could chew, and that now he was paying the price with his sanity.

Everything Lannister Ravenclaw had worked toward was crumbling around him, and all he was able to do was sit in his bedchamber and wince in pain while those damned voices reverberated through his mind. Finally, the combination of everything, the voices, the pain, the failure, all became so unbearable, so suffocating, that Lannister Ravenclaw cried out to whatever unnatural force had cursed him. He fell to his hands and knees on the floor of his bedchamber, and screamed "What is it?! What in the hells do you want from me?!"

In that instant, it stopped. The pain, the chanting, both vanished. Lannister looked about the room nervously, fearing some demon would appear to put him out of his misery. Cautiously, the halfling stood up, and was greeted by a single, booming voice in his mind. The voice spoke in a monotone, as had his patron, but this voice was different, almost dense, as if all the voices that had plagued Lannister's mind were all speaking as one. "Time is dwindling, Guildmaster Ravenclaw." the voice spoke "You have not been faithful to the Mission."

"What do you mean?" Lannister pleaded in response. "I've done all I can! Those smugglers are the best I know, they never fail on a job."

"Time is dwindling." the voice repeated "Your smugglers have not proven expedient enough for the sake of the Mission. It is to be assumed that they have failed."

"Well what do you want me to do about it?" Lannister cried out in anger and frustration.

"Go to Hallowspire; find the elf and bring it to Lohvast."

"Are you mad?" Lannister hissed "Do you know what I am? If I'm spotted in Hallowspire they'll put me down like a rabid dog!"

All of the sudden, pain returned to the halfling's shoulder, an intense searing pain like the one he felt when he first received the brand, only amplified tenfold. He cried out in pain and fell back into the chair he had been sitting in. "You possess a training in stealth and discretion that few achieve. You can infiltrate Hallowspire undetected. Your reservation is unacceptable. Go to Hallowspire. Find the elf."

"Alright, alright! I'll do it, I'll do anything! I'll stay true to the Mission, please!"

In that instant, the pain once again left Lannister's shoulder. In his mind, he heard the voice, now cleft in twain, echo.

"So has it been said,"
"So has it been heard,"
"So has it been understood,"
"So shall it be done."

After that, the voices were gone, and so too was Lannister Ravenclaw, who that night took a pony from the Guildhall stables, and began to ride fervently toward Hallowspire.

CHAPTER EIGHTEEN

O nce Enna had become comfortable in, or at least accepting of her present surroundings, it became evident that the purpose of Varis' constant presence was that he meant to educate her and Erasmus. The lessons began with a study of the elven language. A complex language by nature, and so unlike the plain speech of the Kingdoms, Enna had a difficult time understanding the intricacies of even the simplest phrases, often becoming frustrated, and more than once asking Varis what the point was of such exercises.

"This is pointless," she once claimed in exasperation, staring at what to her looked like a parchment of gibberish "I mean, when in my life am I going to need to know the Elvish alphabet, let alone the words for the elements?"

"It will make sense in time." Varis reassured her. "For now, think of this as a constructive way to pass the time whilst in your present situation."

Erasmus helped whenever he could with said lessons, as his life as a bard had taught him many things, such as knowing enough Elvish to get by when the need arose. "These overlapping lines show compounded letters." he explained, pointing at the parchment. "Here, you have earth, *kemen*, and here, water, *alu*." The half-elf moved his finger across the letters, demonstrating how the lines fit together phonetically.

"Oh..." Enna nodded "I think I understand." She traced over the next set of letters with her finger, as Erasmus had done. "Wind..." she said, looking at the word written in plain letters over top the Elvish script "Sul..."

"Very good." Varis said approvingly "And fire?"

"Wait a minute..." Enna paused, thinking. "'A amin I' sul... Varis, that's what I said when I cast that spell during market day."

"That makes sense," Varis nodded "Elvish is the arcane tongue."

"Yeah, I've always wondered about that." Erasmus mentioned offhandedly.

"I mean, I clearly don't know Elvish, how would I know to say those words?"

"Most human casters have no idea what any of the spells mean," Erasmus offered "I'm sure plenty don't even know what language the spells are in when they learn them."

"But I never learned anything." Enna contested "My parents are farmers, all I ever learned was how to live as a farmer. Even knowing how to read and write plain letters comes from my father being a merchant before I was born."

"Do not worry about such matters right now." Varis calmly tried to get the two back on track. "I will answer those questions on another day. For now," he said, tapping a slender finger onto the parchment "fire."

***

On the evening of the fifth day since Enna and Erasmus had been imprisoned, Varis sat with them following a supper of the same root stew as the last four days. Enna was beginning to grasp Elvish better, albeit only in the sense that while she was now able to read words aloud, she was more often than not unable to equate those words to their Common counterparts. Varis had said little during the meal, spending the majority of it looking as though he was planning on saying something, but unsure of the best phrasing. Finally, after a long period of contemplation, Varis spoke to Enna and Erasmus.

"The other day, questions were asked." he began. "There is no sense in delaying their answer any further." He turned to Erasmus, "Tell me, what do you know of the Four Kingdoms?"

Erasmus ran a hand over his dark goatee, thinking a moment. "I know that the nobility of Lohvast have deep pockets for a good bard." he smirked "I know that the Half-Orc cities are the only things keeping Majadrin trading with Ghest, who has the most beautiful women, by the way." Enna rolled her eyes while Varis listened stoically. "And I know, thanks to you, that Hallowspire doesn't care for visitors because the

King's a puppet for a xenophobic Archmage." he counted the tidbits of information out on one hand as he spoke. "I'm sure there's more, but I only take note of the important things."

Varis nodded. "There is more, indeed, Erasmus. All you have done, as I suspected you might, was to explain one of the Four Kingdoms: the Kingdom of Earth."

"I don't understand." Enna looked curiously at Varis.

"As neither of you should." Varis stated. "You were both, I can assume, raised by human parents?" both nodded. "So then neither one of you would ever have been told what you are about to hear. You are both aware, of course, of the existence of the great dwarven cities to the south, as well as east of Majadrin? Well, think a moment; you both are aware of the existence of elves, as well as other fae beings, and yet I imagine neither of you could name a great elven city."

"I had always assumed that elves were a lot of nomadic loners." Erasmus shrugged.

"This is because your elven parent never told you of your heritage?"

"He would have had to have been present to have done so." Erasmus' words had the slightest hint of venom.

"Oh, Erasmus, I'm so sorry..." Enna began, prompting the half-elf to wave away the words.

"Old wounds, long since healed." he said dismissively. "Continue, Varis."

"The reason that the existence of any great fae cities is unknown to the both of you is because of something that we fae races do not speak of to anyone outside of ourselves. The fact that there are four mortal kingdoms happens to be an excellent coincidence to cover up the real Four Kingdoms: the Kingdoms of Earth, Stone, Wood, and Fire."

"What does all of this have to do with what Erasmus and I had asked before?" Enna interjected "About arcana, and Elvish, and how I knew what to say to cast a spell?"

"To understand that," Varis continued "You must understand the Four Kingdoms. The Kingdom of Earth is the domain of the mortal races, called so due to their relatively short lifespans. It is the kingdom of humans, of halflings, orcs and goblins. The Kingdom of Stone is the domain of dwarves and of giants, made up of the mountains and hills deemed impassable by the mortal races, and the labyrinthine caverns below them. Earth and Stone are the Kingdoms of the Mortal realm, and as such are not inherently arcane in the least."

"So that leaves Wood and Fire." Enna stated.

"I take it the Kingdom of Wood is the elven domain?" Erasmus asked.

Varis nodded. "Indeed, the Kingdom of Wood is something of a colloquialism for the fae realm as a whole, another place entirely from this realm, reachable only by those with knowledge of arcana greater than even the Archmages, for it is here from whence arcane power is drawn."

"What do you mean?" Enna asked.

"When someone casts an arcane spell, what they are doing is drawing energy from the fae realm, displacing it temporarily in this realm to be bent to the caster's will. This is why Elvish is the language of arcana."

"Can the process be reversed?" Erasmus asked "In the fae realm, do they draw on energy from this realm?"

Varis shook his head. "The fae realm is inherently arcane, pulsing with powerful energies; fae beings are naturally imbued with them."

"And what about the Kingdom of Fire?" Enna asked, trying to take in all this new information.

"The Kingdom of Fire is a place of demons." Varis said gravely "It is known as the infernal realm, and is the origin point of sorcery, a destructive force similar to arcana, but brought forth by power hungry individuals, twisted souls who make pacts with the demons of the realm, often gaining great power, but at the price of being the demon's puppet servant."

"Why is this the first I'm hearing of all of this?" Erasmus asked. "I mean, everyone hears the stories about evil demons, and about fae-folk carrying you away in the night to some magical place, but I'm half-fae, and I've met plenty of elves and gnomes in my life, not one of them telling me anything like this."

"When a fae being decides to cross over to the mortal realm, he or she swears an oath never to discuss the Four Kingdoms, nor the nature of arcana and of sorcery with mortal beings. Though you are half-elf, Erasmus, you have a human name, and carry yourself in a manner that is indicative that you had a decidedly human upbringing."

"That's fair enough, I suppose," Erasmus conceded "but then, why explain all this to the two of us? And for that matter, what does all of this have to do with Enna being able to cast spells?"

Varis held out his left wrist, revealing the tattoo Enna had spotted before. "When I was thrown in this prison on charges of heresy, I was to be executed. Instead, Archmage Tyn saw me as an asset, and offered me a bargain: my life would be spared if I could design some means of disabling a person's ability to cast spells. With my knowledge, I was able to construct this: a powerful warding glyph, blocking the wearer's connection to the fae realm, and thus disabling their ability to channel energy from it. When we met, I had told you of three arcanists who had been deemed 'reeducated' and released. Each of those three agreed to receive one of these tattoos, ensuring that they would no longer be a 'threat' to Hallowspire. As per the Archmage's orders."

"That didn't answer his question..." Enna said, all of the sudden filled with dread "Are you planning on tattooing us with those?"

"Absolutely not." Varis answered. "I had a drunk and a whore from the common prisons take your places some time ago; they were released thereafter."

Enna's eyes widened. "Does that mean we're free to go?" she gasped.

"In theory I could discreetly send you both on your way, and none would be the wiser." Varis replied "However in reality there are reasons I must keep you here."

"What do you mean?" Erasmus asked, growing impatient with the elf's roundabout speech "Why are you keeping us here, Varis?"

"Of all the arcanists who have been arrested in Hallowspire in the last thirty years," Varis looked pointedly to Enna "all but two have been mortal."

Enna stared blankly at Varis, as Erasmus' eyes widened with the realization. "Wait..." Enna began "What are you saying?"

"Your parents, that is to say, your adoptive human parents, did an impeccable job of hiding your lineage, Enna, and in their defense I doubt you would be sitting here today were it not for that fact; the King's Guard have a history of being notoriously...*callous* when dealing with fae children."

Enna reflexively reached up and clasped the tops of her ears, running her fingers along the scarring. Her parents *did* that to her? On purpose? Why would they lie to her for all those years? Who were her real parents? Enna's chest all of the sudden began to feel very heavy, and her breathing became laboured. Varis extended an arm, resting his hand on Enna's shoulder. "I am sure this is much to take in..."

Enna swatted the elf's hand away "Don't touch me." she growled "You're lying, it's a lie!" she tried to leap from her chair at Varis, only to have Erasmus grab at her shoulders to try and restrain her. She thrashed and protested, but couldn't escape the half-elf's grasp.

"Easy, Enna. Just calm down." Erasmus, feeling Enna was no longer resisting, eased up on her as she sank back into her chair. He looked over to Varis "You had better go."

Varis nodded "Perhaps it is best if I give you time to absorb everything that we spoke of tonight." As he gathered the platters from supper and headed for the door, Enna's eyes bore into him with an anger not born of hatred, but of confusion and surprise. "I shall return tomorrow, however, as ever. I am sure you will have plenty of questions."

That night, Enna tossed and turned, her mind alight with so many questions, none of which she ever thought she would have, and none of which she wanted answered. Erasmus, on the other hand, tossed and turned, his mind alight with the realization that the mysterious elf whom he and O'doc had been paid to take to Lannister Ravenclaw was not some criminal or rival or deadbeat, but rather was a young girl who, in less than a week, had everything she had ever known crumble right before her eyes.

***

The next day Enna had returned to her previous state of not talking. This was different from before, however, as her silence now was less an act of anger and spite, and more contemplative in nature. She spoke when spoken to, though often her responses were brief and dismissive. Other than that, she simply sat, lost in her own thoughts. It did not help that Erasmus, someone who in the last few days Enna had begun to see as a friend, and had even grown to trust, seemed slightly distant, as if something plagued his thoughts as well.

Varis had come with breakfast that morning, but did not eat with the pair, or even stay, stating only that he would return later. He did, however, leave a rolled-up parchment. After finishing breakfast, Enna took the scroll and unrolled it, revealing two pages. The first was a note that read:

Enna,

I apologize for the callousness with which I revealed the nature of your birth yesterday. In hindsight, the matter could have been handled with far greater delicacy on my part. While I can understand that you will no doubt rather not have my company at this time, I do still encourage you and Erasmus to continue your studies. Enclosed is a page with words and phrases I feel you would be comfortable with. I will continue to operate as such until you both are comfortable with my presence once more. I hope to continue these lessons face-to-face sooner, rather than later.

Respectfully,

Varis Liadon

The second page was, as the first had described, a sheet full of words and phrases in plain letters, with their spelling in Elvish underneath. Enna took both sheets and slid them to the centre of the table, proceeding then to get up and walk toward her sleeping quarters. Erasmus, curious, looked at the pages, reading the note carefully. He replaced the parchment, and walked over to Enna, who was looking down, washing her hands in her basin.

"My mother never told me who my father was."

Enna remained silent, still washing.

"I mean, I'm sure she had her reasons, but that didn't make it easy... Bad enough being called a bastard by the other children, but a half-blooded bastard?" Erasmus shook his head. "It made me angry, all of it. I got into a lot of fights. Part of the problem with being a half-elf is that neither side is all that willing to claim you as one of their own.

Humans, the rural ones mostly, almost always see you as an elf, come to cast spells and whisk away their young. You're unwanted and untrusted. Meanwhile, the elves tend to be a bit more accepting, provided you either conform completely to the elven lifestyle or otherwise stay at arm's length.

"Maybe that's why I took to living in cities" he mused "more often than not there's such a hodgepodge of people that I could sit down and play cards with a dwarf, two elves, and a half-orc, and not one would bat an eyelash at another, unless someone was cheating. Funny thing is, that probably wouldn't have been the case if not for my mother." Enna looked up at the half-elf as he stood reminiscing. "Mom always loved having music in the house; she gave me my mandolin, Caster, and I spent hours, days at a time learning all the old lullabies she would sing to me. Funny thing is, from what I understand, a lot of them were old Elvish lullabies. Still some of my favourite things to play..."

"You named your mandolin?" Enna smirked.

"Of course! An instrument with no name has no character." Erasmus began to walk to his own quarters "And I like my ladies to have plenty of character."

Enna began to walk back to the table, sitting down in her chair and pulling the parchments in front of her. Her parents, her human parents, raised Enna to always see things through. Indeed, Enna was a Summerlark, and she knew that would never change. She knew now, also, that she was an elf by blood, and though it was a part of her that she had gone her whole life knowing nothing about, she was now determined to find out all she could.

Erasmus sat on his bed, wondering what he was going to do. Some way, somehow, he had every intention of leaving Rheth a free man, but then what? It was becoming more and more apparent that Enna was the elf that he and O'doc were to deliver, and yet Erasmus could find no reason in his mind to turn her over to the Rats. He reasoned that there must be some reason why she was so important, but he doubted she even knew why. From across the way, Erasmus heard Enna at the table.

"Good day...quel re. Good evening...quel lome."

The half-elf smirked in spite of himself, and in that moment knew that he wanted no part in whatever heinous designs Lannister

Ravenclaw had for the poor girl ,and decided that if there were some kind of secret about Enna Summerlark that no one knew, he was willing to help her find out.

CHAPTER NINETEEN

Most of the physical features of the prisons below Rheth, such as the width and height of doors and hallways, were designed to be most easily accessible to humans, a fact that proved to be a great hindrance for a dwarf and a halfling attempting to traverse them. Many design oversights, however, such as the dimly lit corridors, and the throngs of unoccupied cells, served the purposes of the two escapees quite well. Indeed, the very fact that the prison complex was underground was quite to the liking of Adrik Thornmallet, who in spite of spending much of his life above ground and on the road was still innately acclimated to subterranean settings. Taking the lead more often than not, the dwarf was able to see and hear much better than his halfling companion, and by that account much better than any of the King's Guard who may be patrolling just around the next corner, giving the two ample warning if they were required to dart into the shadows, or even an empty cell, if necessary. What's more, Adrik's sense of direction, honed from a lifetime spent traversing subterranean dwarven cities, allowed the two to maintain their bearings at all times. There remained, however, one glaring problem in the pair's escape attempt: in spite of Adrik's instinctual compass, the two nonetheless had no idea where they were going. It was a fact that O'doc made a point of mentioning to Adrik at the turn of roughly every third corner, or barring that, after passing through every door.

"We are lost!" O'doc said in a hoarse whisper, trying as discreetly as possible to close the two into another empty cell "I feel like we've been twisting through these foul corridors for hours now. Do you have any kind of plan, any idea where we're going?"

Adrik shrugged. "I know where we have been, and where we

have not. In all truth, I had been hoping that you would have developed some kind of strategy by now."

"Me?! You were the one who head-butted that guard and got us into this situation!"

"I saw an opportunity for our egress, and I seized it."

"That you did, and now we're running like maniacs, hoping not to get caught trying to escape!"

"By the sounds of things, your strategy would have resulted in an identical scenario, albeit at a much later date."

There was a self-assured nonchalance about the dwarf that was beginning to grate on O'doc, partially because of the present situation, and partially because it reminded him of Erasmus. "Well maybe if you'd have given me the extra four days I could have figured out a better plan then 'oh, I hear a sound, let's dive into another rat-infested cell!'"

"Well now would be an optimal time for such planning." Adrik placed his hand on O'doc's shoulder "Perhaps if you were to take some deep breaths and calm yourself; a calm mind is far more conducive to creative thought, you know."

Before O'doc could explode in a fit of frustration, the pair heard the bang of a pole arm on the cell door. "Right then," a Guard shouted at them "What're the pair 'o you whispering about?"

As if on cue, O'doc turned and walked up to the cell door, feigning a drunken stumble, and looked up at the Guard with over blinking eyes. "That lousy dwarf..." he slurred "Stole my chick'n! How's a man s'pposed to feed 'is family if he's gotta worry about chick'n thieving... thieves... dwarves takin' things aren't belong to them?"

Adrik, following the halfling's lead, let forth a loud belch. "Now you see here!" he said as he stumbled up to O'doc, turning as well to face the Guard "It was this ruffian halfling who went and took *my* chicken! He told me she wasn't for sale, but I knew we had something special she'd have been my pet... my best friend..." Adrik then proceeded to collapse at his companion's feet, mock sobbing "Oh, poor Marnia... All I wanted was a better life for you, one that wouldn't end with you on some chopping block... Daddy's failed you, girl!"

"Oh, pipe down, the both of you!" the Guard bellowed, hitting her pole arm against the door once again. "Keep it up and I'll shackle you up!" The Guard then proceeded to march off, mumbling something under her breath about "lousy drunks and their stupid fights."

Once the Guard was out of earshot, Adrik hopped to his feet and dusted himself off. "A fine showing, good sir!" he grinned "You would make a fine merchant out on the road."

"Well my current career seems to be looking less appealing by the day." O'doc sighed, having slightly calmed down "And the Gods know if I botch this current job, I'll likely need a new career, if not a whole new identity..."

"Your present employer is a particularly unforgiving individual, I gather?"

"That is an understatement if ever I heard one..." O'doc quickly tried to shift his thoughts away from those of an angry Lannister Ravenclaw "Enough about that, though; we need a plan."

"Well, judging by where that Guard was headed, I surmise that the opposite direction would be an optimal destination for us." Adrik stroked his beard as he thought. "From there, it would likely be most advantageous to head generally northward."

"How do you figure?"

"It is safe to assume that these prisons are relatively below Castle Rheth. Being as that is the case, and accounting for the fact that both your arrest and mine took place south of the castle, one can ascertain that in order to find your companion and mine, we had best delve deeper into these catacombs."

O'doc stared blankly at the dwarf for a moment, unable to believe what he had just heard. "You want us to rescue Erasmus, and Randis' daughter?"

"Undoubtedly. What were your intentions?"

"To escape! To lie low in some tavern here in Rheth until I was able to get word from Erasmus."

"My dear sir, for shame!" Adrik's tone became stern "You would allow your compatriot and mine to suffer the fate of two fae beings caught in the prisons of the Great Bastion of Man?"

"Erasmus is clever, he'd no doubt find some way of charming himself free, and besides, he's only half..." O'doc paused, and looked at Adrik suspiciously "Wait, what do you mean 'two fae beings?'"

Adrik, fearing he had said too much, and taking note of the look in O'doc's eye, attempted to assuage any implications on his part. "I meant only that the two were *arrested* under charges that pertain to arcana and fae beings alike, and that knowing the insufferable intolerance of this place they will be all the worse off if we sit by idly."

"Maybe you're right..." O'doc said hesitantly "I think I have a plan: our best bet is to look for doors with locks. It would make sense that they'd be more likely to lead out of here, and we still have the keys from that Guard you knocked out."

"Good show, sir." Adrik clapped the halfling on the shoulder "I shall lead us forth, to rescue. What ho!"

O'doc was unsure of what Adrik had meant about the Summerlark girl, but he knew two things as he followed the dwarf down the corridors: there was something about the girl worth investigating, and Adrik Thornmallet was a willing, if unknowing guide, helping O'doc find out just what that thing was.

The pair continued on their way through the winding corridors, ducking into shadowy corners and dank cells when necessary. Eventually, as O'doc had predicted, they came upon a large wood door with an iron keyhole. Listening keenly both down the hall and at the door to ensure there were no approaching steps, Adrik signaled to the halfling to try the keys. After fumbling with a few, O'doc managed to find the key which fit the door, and proceeded to open it as quietly as possible. The area that lay beyond the door was pitch black, prompting Adrik to lead the way as O'doc removed the key and closed the door behind them.

"What do you see?" O'doc whispered, reaching out to find that the walls on either side of him were closer than even the narrowest passages the two had traversed up to this point.

"Not nearly as much as would be preferred..." Adrik's eyes, though attuned to darkness, were only able to penetrate the blackness as well as a human's eyes could penetrate the thick of a nighttime fog. The dwarf held his hands out and began to step cautiously, eventually seeing what appeared to be a shelf in front of him. "It would appear that we have happened upon some manner of supplies lockup." he said, reaching for what looked like a candle and some flint. Striking the flint on the ground, Adrik was able to light the candle, bathing the room in a dim, soft glow, just barely bright enough for the pair to both see that there was more within it than just supplies.

O'doc's eyes lit up at the sight of piles of haphazardly tossed goods. Everything from weapons and agricultural tools to ornate flagons and trivial knick-knacks littered the floor, surrounded by shelves of better organized goods, likely supplies for the Guard. "Some of the guards must have brought their confiscated goods here..." he said half to himself.

"Supplies would certainly not go unwarranted, should a scenario in which to use them happen to present itself."

Adrik was barely through his sentence before O'doc went to work sifting through the small horde. Still trying his best to be discreet, the halfling found a pair of traveler's sacks on one of the shelves and proceeded to fill them with whatever looked most valuable, often small gold or gem-encrusted items. He came across a pair of daggers in ornate leather sheathes, each with some manner of Elvish writing along them. He took the weapons and fastened them to his belt. "All manner of arms here," he said, looking back at Adrik "what's your pleasure?"

Adrik approached the pile. "I never was one to take to the more martial pursuits..." he said as he looked, spotting a small mace which had for its head a depiction of a gnarled tree with a wizened old face. He picked up the weapon and smirked at O'doc. "Mind you, were I to find myself in a bind, I would not be adverse to the use of something similar to this."

Continuing his search, O'doc caught out of the corner of his eye a familiar leather case. He immediately snatched it up, proceeding to unclasp it and inspect its contents. "She looks to be in good shape..." he said, running one hand along the body of Erasmus' mandolin.

"Ah, what luck for us that we shall be able to reunite your bard with his muse!" Adrik grinned, holding out a hand "Give it here, friend; my sack is as of yet largely unoccupied." The two gathered up a handful more items: a pair of short swords, a jewel-topped club, and a few more objects that O'doc deemed worth the effort to carry. The pair slung the packs over their shoulders, and walked quietly toward the entrance. Adrik once again listened at the door while O'doc snuffed out the candle, once again covering the room in darkness.

After several moments, Adrik began to open the door, confident that there was no stirring on the other side. The pair crept out and closed the door, locking it behind them. Just as they turned to walk away, O'doc caught something in his periphery that caused him to stop dead; someone was emerging, silent as death, from a shadowy alcove just on the other side of the hall. He put a hand on Adrik, who turned around just in time to see a tall, aged elf standing not five feet from them.

"Well, well..." the elf said, eying the two stoically. "This will complicate matters."

CHAPTER TWENTY

Varis strolled into Enna and Erasmus' chamber, platters of stew in one hand, and something tucked underneath the opposite arm. Enna sat, continuing to read from the parchment Varis had left earlier, while Erasmus got up to help the visibly struggling elf. Erasmus reached out both hands, taking the platter from Varis, only to notice that the other object Varis was carrying with him looked very familiar. Erasmus' eyes went wide, and he hurriedly placed the platter on the table before rushing back over to the elf, unable to contain his anxiousness. "By the Gods, that isn't what I think it is, is it?" Erasmus nearly yanked the leather case from Varis as it was passed to him.

Walking it over to the table, Erasmus placed the case down more gingerly than if it had been made of thinly blown glass. Hands shaking, fearing the condition of the contents, the half-elf opened the clasps on the case, pulling the top flap back to reveal the dark-lacquered cedar body and rosewood fretboard with gold glyph inlays. Running one hand across the instrument, it seemed to be unblemished. Nervously, Erasmus took the mandolin by the neck and lifted it from the case, turning it over in his hands, looking closely at every nook, cranny, and crevasse in its body. Finally, apparently satisfied with its condition, Erasmus propped his left foot onto one of the wooden chairs, sitting the mandolin across the flat of his thigh. He clasped the neck with his left hand, placing each finger into a practiced position, raised his right hand and strummed a chord.

The sound was that came forth was a dissonant, atonal mess that caused all three in the room to involuntarily cringe at the noise. "Sorry, I guess she's out of tune..." Erasmus said sheepishly, before adjusting a handful of the tuning keys. Giving the chord a second try, the mandolin produced a beautiful sound. "Oh, Caster..." Erasmus stroked the mandolin lovingly "thought I'd gone and lost you forever." He looked up at Varis "Where did you find her? What can I offer you in return?"

Varis raised his hand to stop the half-elf. "No repayment is necessary, Erasmus. I wish for the two of you to be my protégées, after all, and what good would it have done me to have come upon your implement and not return it to you?"

"You mean to make us your protégées?" Enna asked, looking up from her parchment.

"Certainly." Varis answered "It is why I kept you both safe, and kept your whereabouts unknown to the Archmage." he walked toward the table and stood opposite Erasmus "I have rendered myself unable to cast spells, this is true, but it is a knowledge that I have an obligation to pass onto others that are of the fae realm, that you might be keepers, arbiters of its power. This is why elves have come to the mortal realm for so many generations" Varis looked to Erasmus, then to Enna "I imagine it is why your father, and your birth parents arrived here."

"What do you mean by arbiters?" Erasmus asked.

"The powers of arcana are far too great for their secrets to be revealed to the mortal races. When humans find anything that grants them power, they abuse it, having no foresight or thought of consequences."

"Not all humans are like that." Enna said defensively.

"No," Varis was ever-stoic "but enough are irresponsible enough to allow those who would abuse arcana to do so. Why else would these individuals turn to sorcery?"

"I'll grant you that," Erasmus said "but say you teach us to control arcane power, what's to say we don't use that power and blast our way out of here?"

"Before I tattooed this glyph onto myself" Varis began, rolling back his sleeve to once again show the tattoo on his wrist "I placed it within the mortar work of a number of rooms, this one included. No arcane spells may be cast here, as the glyphs are bound to my own, and thus are bound to my life."

"Well what's the point of all this, then?" Erasmus asked confusedly "And for that matter, you still haven't told me where you found my mandolin."

"Your implement, oddly enough, was discovered through pure happenstance. I was on my way to fetch your supper, when I came across a halfling and a dwarf sneaking out of a supply room. The two tried to run from me, but I was able to seize them easily enough. Judging from their looks, I could assume that they were prisoners who had escaped; not an easy task. I brought them to another of my rooms, similar to his one. I get the feeling that they could be more than they seem."

"I think that might be O'doc and Adrik!" Enna exclaimed. "Those are our friends!" she turned to Erasmus "do you think that they were trying to find us?"

"That would explain the mandolin." Varis nodded. "Very well, if they are indeed your friends, I shall whisk them outside Rheth under the cover of night. I know of a path in these corridors that leads to just outside the city walls, and from there they may go where they please."

"Wait, what about us, then?" Enna asked.

"You are to remain here."

"For how long?"

"As long as is necessary for whomever is on the Hallowspire throne at that time to come to their senses. Elves are a vigorous and long-living people, and I have heard many half-elves share that trait. In many ways, we have nothing but time."

"And what of the people of Hallowspire?" Erasmus cried out. "You've told us what's happened over the course of the last three decades, who knows how much worse it could get if you keep sitting here doing nothing."

"What of them?" Varis began to walk toward Erasmus, a venom to his tone. "The mortal races are short-lived and short-sighted. You are proof of that; raised by humans and bred to be a lowly minstrel, using your gift to do no more that trick people into giving you a bit more coin. How you even deign to look me in the eye and pretend to care for the people of this Kingdom, in *any* of the mortal kingdoms, is beyond my comprehension. These people will tear each other apart, Erasmus, and it is our charge to ensure that they do so without pulling apart our home as they do."

Before Varis could continue, his thoughts were interrupted by the large metal platter he had brought in, being swung into the back of his head by Enna, and thus falling down unconscious as a result. Erasmus looked up at the girl "Nice swing."

"Years of chopping wood'll do that." she smirked. "I say we take his keys and go find our friends." she looked down at Varis "I may be an elf, but I hope to the gods I never think like that one."

CHAPTER TWENTY-ONE

In his opulent bedchamber, Derrus Tyn sat meditating. In some ways, he had been quite pleased with how the week since the incidents on market day had progressed; the two rogue arcanists had been dispatched, their abettors no doubt withering in a cell below castle Rheth. The King's Guard were quickly rounding up any potential arcane implements scattered throughout the city, and would no doubt be working their way to the surrounding towns within the next few days, all with far less backlash than the Archmage suspected. Even King Renton had seemed sufficiently placated, even pleased by Tyn's work. Regardless, however, the Archmage could not sit on his laurels, for there was still the Mission. He had still made little progress in the merger of Hallowspire and Lohvast, as pressing the issue only ever fouled the King's mood. Further, there was still the matter of the purported elf; for so long Tyn had successfully thwarted the reemergence of fae-folk in Hallowspire, kept them from inherently interfering with the Mission. If even one were to emerge, their potential impact would be devastating. Yet, the rumours floated, and as such could not be ignored. The Mission was paramount, and any fae presence, even whispered rumours, could not be left unchecked.

The Archmage's thoughts were interrupted by the sound of his bedchamber door opening behind him. "Unless I bid you enter," he snapped, eyes still closed "you've no reason to be doing anything other than keeping watch at my door!" After a moment of utter silence, Tyn turned around to see the Guard who had been assigned to watch his door, eyes and mouth wide, apparently gasping for air, before falling to the floor in a dead heap. A small, shadowy figure stood behind the body, proceeding to bend over and pull a dagger from the Guard's back.

Stepping into the candlelight, the figure revealed itself to be rodent-like, dressed in clothes that seemed slightly too big for it. "You know," the figure said in a high-pitched voice, wiping the dagger off on its shirt "there's a chink in those back plates where you can slide a blade right into their lungs. Worked for about five of them out in the halls, and that one right there."

Tyn leaped up from his sitting position, turning on his heels. He clasped at a golden amulet hanging from his neck with his right hand, and reached out toward the figure with his left. He cried out in a low reverberant voice

"TESSA SINA ONNA"

The figure attempted to do a backward handspring defensively, but halfway through the maneuver seemed to stiffen, as if some great invisible hand had clasped around it, causing it to tumble to the ground, trying to writhe its way free.

Tyn approached the struggling figure, who began to change form before his very eyes. Its hair thinned, its muzzle receded into its face, and its figure took on the form of a male halfling. There was something about the apparent were-rat that the Archmage could not quite discern, something that differentiated him from an average lycanthrope. "Who are you, and how did you find your way into this castle, much less my chambers?"

"You don't know?" the halfling answered, looking up at the robed man standing over him. "Isn't that novel. Look, dispel this hold you have on me and I can explain."

"Why should I trust some filthy lycanthrope that managed to kill six King's Guard?"

"Look at me right now," the halfling responded incredulously "I made no act of aggression toward you, and yet here I lie like a trout on some toothless fishmonger's cart. Even if I was stupid enough to try and attack an Archmage, which I am not, why would I have announced my entrance as I did?"

"You could be lying to win my trust."

"If I was, then you'd likely incinerate me before I could get anywhere near you." The halfling wriggled about some more "now unbind me, already; I'm here because of the Mission."

~ 95 ~

The Archmage furrowed his brow, and with an almost dismissive wave of his hand released the halfling. "I am waiting for an explanation." he said expectantly.

The halfling hopped up to his feet and rocked his head from side to side, cracking the joints in his neck, and then bowing low "Lannister Ravenclaw, Guildmaster of the River Rats, as requested, at your service."

"I never requested you." Tyn said suspiciously. "What do you know of the Mission?"

"Oh? You didn't eh?"

"I have no idea who you are, nor why you are here."

"Then would you mind explaining this?" Ravenclaw pulled open his shirt, revealing the mark on his shoulder.

Tyn's eyes widened; that explained the strange feeling he had about the halfling from the onset. "You were marked..." he half-whispered.

"You mean to tell me that all those arcane meetings, all that talk about 'the Mission', the entire plan to have me send bounty hunters out here to find your missing elf... that wasn't you?" Ravenclaw gave a dry laugh "You paid me in Hallowspire coin! How stupid do you think I am?"

"I was not the one who contacted you, you filthy rogue!" Tyn snapped "The Mission is far greater than I alone. We are all but Vessels for Its Voice. We have been granted boons, and as such we are in Its debt. When It spoke to you, it would have been through any one of us, and none of us would have any recollection. You were likely paid with this kingdom's coin because it left little trail for you to follow, because you were only supposed to be a means to an end." He looked Ravenclaw up and down. "For whatever reason, it has marked you, allowed you to know of the Mission. Perhaps you, too, have been granted a boon."

"If you want to call voices in my head and dissent among my subordinates a boon that's your prerogative." Ravenclaw sneered, closing his shirt "I'm here because it appears that my mercenaries failed in their task, or got killed trying, and now I've got no choice but to deal with this bloody elf of yours myself."

It was at that moment that another King's Guard came rushing into the room. He looked as though he were poised to say something, but stopped dead at the sight of the body on the floor. "Well?" Tyn cried out across the room when the Guard remained silent and staring "What is it?"

The Guard, jostled back into his thoughts, gave a short bow. "Archmage Tyn, there is a situation that requires your attention."

"I am aware of it, and I assure you that nothing is amiss; clear away the six bodies however is most effective, make sure you remove their armour, and ensure that there is no visible blood."

The Guard looked confused. "Clear away the... No, sir, I mean, immediately, sir, but there is another situation, in the prisons."

"Oh?" Tyn replied testily "And what might that situation be?"

"Two of the prisoners, sir. They escaped several hours ago. Kroft found Ratley gagged and shackled in the cell, his keys had been stolen."

The Archmage placed two fingers on each temple and began to massage them. "What prisoners were in that cell?" he growled.

"A dwarf and a halfling, sir, the ones brought in with the human and half-elf arcanists a week ago."

Tyn stormed up to the nervous guard, breathing hotly on him. "Scour the castle!" he screamed "Use every man and woman you can find!" The guard nodded quickly before running out of the room. Ravenclaw walked up beside the Archmage, a wide, yellowed smirk playing across his face. "What are you smiling about?" Tyn said.

"Because I think I might know that halfling." Ravenclaw said looking up at Tyn, still grinning. "And if I do, you're in hells more trouble than you think you are."

CHAPTER TWENTY-TWO

Adrik Thornmallet threw his shoulder against the large wooden door to the room in which he and O'doc Overhill were being kept. It no more gave way on this particular attempt than it had in all the combined attempts of the last hour. The dwarf's shoulder ached, and his legs had begun to cramp on account of the repeated running starts taken toward the door. O'doc, meanwhile, was inspecting his now broken lock pick.

"In hindsight of recent events" Adrik said as he walked back toward the halfling, massaging his tender shoulder "I am sufficiently more satisfied with my decision not to wait for your plan."

"This pick has never failed me, not in the five years since I started using it."

"Well perhaps it had reached an expiration." the dwarf countered, before running once more into the door, again to no avail. "By Othar's beard, this is starting to sting!" Adrik walked to a nearby chair and sat on it, wincing in pain. "Perhaps that pick of yours simply realized the futility of its efforts and simply broke of its own despair."

"The Gods damn that elf." O'doc sighed. "I don't understand it, in all the places in the Four Kingdoms why would an elf be wandering around here?"

"That was Varis Liadon, former Archmage of Hallowspire." Adrik said, still wincing as he tried to lift his sore arm. "I was under the assumption that he had been tried for treason, and that he had been either privately executed some three decades ago, or that he was, as we speak, locked away in recesses far deeper than what you and I had endured. Evidently the former Archmage appears to still be actively serving the Crown in some manner."

O'doc looked at Adrik blankly. "How do you know all that?"

Adrik gave a short, pained chuckle. "In my occupation, my good man, one keeps abreast of all the political happenings in the lands, it is simply good business practice."

"So if he was a working for the King, why are we in here, and not just back in a cell, and why did he leave all our things with us?"

"Regrettably the gossip mongers about Hallowspire have been significantly less talkative regarding that particular bit."

"Well," O'doc said, returning to his lock pick "whatever his motives are, the fact that we're locked up anywhere puts them at odds with ours." The halfling looked at his tool and sighed once more, then proceeded toward the door. "Might as well give this another try."

"Is it not broken in two?"

"It is," O'doc said as he looked into the keyhole and began to feed the lock pick in with both hands "but another slam into that door and you'll likely be no better, and if we're being honest my lock pick will not serve much good helping me knock out any King's Guard if need should arise." O'doc tried his best to maneuver the lock pick about, feeling for the necessary spots in the mechanism, when he felt something push through the other side of the keyhole, forcing the broken pieces out and onto the floor. O'doc somersaulted back, poised to lunge, hands on his daggers. "He must be coming back." he whispered to Adrik.

"Indeed." the dwarf whispered back, positioning himself as though he were going to charge the door again. "Much to his disadvantage, I would wager the former Archmage is nary as fortuitous as that damnable door."

The door opened slowly, and only part way. The pair tensed in anticipation until O'doc spotted an all-too-familiar head of straight chestnut hair poke through the door, followed by the accompanying face of Erasmus Stonehand. "O'doc!" the half-elf cried out as he spotted his partner. Erasmus opened the door the remainder of the way to reveal Enna Summerlark standing defensively behind him.

Adrik's grin beamed through his thick black beard as he relaxed his posture. "Milady Enna! What irony should befall us that we should be captured in our attempt to rescue you, only to have you wind up as our saviours."

Greetings were exchanged and introductions made. Adrik explained, loquaciously, what had happened to he and O'doc over the last six days, and Enna did the same regarding she and Erasmus. O'doc went through the bags of equipment that he and Adrik had procured, giving Erasmus the pair of short swords, while Adrik handed Enna the club. "I assumed you might require some means by which to defend yourself" the dwarf said to Enna "and as such I opted to find you something that was not particularly brutish."

"Oh, I don't know," Erasmus replied "from what I've heard the girl knows how to swing an axe."

"Well, to be fair" Enna said as she fastened the club to the belt around her dress "I'm sure splitting wood is a bit different than splitting flesh, and I hope I never have to experience the latter. This is perfect, Adrik, thank you." The dwarf gave a low bow, making Enna smile. She was glad to see the dwarf again, for in spite of only having met him on two occasions, there was something comforting about his presence. Counteracting that feeling of comfort, however, was O'doc Overhill. Erasmus had spoken at length to Enna about the halfling, with the kind of affection with which one speaks of a brother, and yet Enna could not shake the feeling that O'doc had been watching her since she and Erasmus found them.

"Alright," Erasmus said, interrupting Enna's thoughts "we got this far, but Enna and I hadn't really thought past this point. I don't think anyone will be looking for me or her, so that should work to our advantage. Anyone have a plan?"

"If we keep our heads down, we could try and make our way back to the prisons." Enna offered "Varis mentioned an escape route he had down there that goes outside the city."

"I fear that may not be an option at this juncture. It would be disingenuous of me to say that our escape was free of loose ends," Adrik frowned "not to say that O'doc and I did not attempt to operate as stealthily as possible, however given how much time has passed now it is not unlikely that the two of us are being sought out." The dwarf turned his gaze to O'doc. "Master O'doc, have you any ideas as to how we might deal with this predicament?"

O'doc began to pace around the room, hand on his chin. "We

don't have many options..." he said, seemingly deep in thought. He began to pass behind Enna, making her slightly uncomfortable. Once the halfling was directly behind her, he stopped and whispered "I am truly sorry." In a flash, O'doc twisted Enna's left hand behind her back and had one of his daggers at her throat.

"Overhill!" Adrik bellowed as he took a step toward the two "By Othar, what are you doing?"

"Nobody move!" O'doc said with a quiver, pressing the flat of the cool blade against Enna's neck.

"O'doc..." Erasmus inched ever so slightly closer to his partner "what are you playing at?"

"I'm doing the job we were hired for!" the halfling shouted back. "This girl is the elf we were supposed to be seeking."

"She's a farm girl," Erasmus protested "she only just found out she wasn't human a few days ago, and barely a handful of people are even aware! We've got no reason to turn her over to Lannister."

"Oh, haven't we?" O'doc let out a dire laugh "you'd sooner deal with the wrath of the River Rats?"

"We can talk to Lannister, tell him..."

"There is no way out of this, Erasmus! You don't know Lannister Ravenclaw, or the River Rats, not like I do..."

Enna's mind raced as the two argued. She wanted to squirm in pain from the arm lock, but the pressure of the dagger kept her still. She tried to think back to market day, to what happened when she accidentally used arcana to save her father. She thought about everything Varis had taught her and Erasmus about how arcana worked, about implements and Elvish and drawing arcane energy from the fae realm. A thought struck her, a risky thought, but one that would hopefully either free her, or distract the halfling long enough for either Adrik or Erasmus to subdue him. Moving as subtly as possible, Enna lifted her free hand up toward her neck until she was able to place it over her pendant. She concentrated, focusing her every thought on what she was trying to imagine. She took a deep, if wavering breath, and in an instant clasped her restrained hand over O'doc's wrist, and shouted an incantation.

"NAUR TULLO' AMIN CAM!"

Enna felt the eldritch energy pulse through her body, exiting through her restrained hand. At once, a searing heat burst forth, causing O'doc to cry out in pain and release his grip on both Enna and the dagger. Erasmus rushed over to hold the halfling's arms behind his back as Enna quickly got out of the way, only to turn back around to face the halfling and half-elf, staring directly at Erasmus with eyes filled with a quiet rage. "What did he mean just now?" her voice was shaking, as much from what had just happened as from a barely restrained anger. "Why did he say that I'm the elf you've been looking for?"

Erasmus stared back at Enna a moment, unsure of what to say. "Enna, I swear that I..."

"Swear that you what?" Enna growled back "That you were planning on telling me I was some *bounty* once you had me tied up in the back of some cart? Or were you planning on charming me so that I just went along willingly to be tortured, or whored, or the Gods know what else?"

"You think I, *we*, knew who you were when we took the job?" Erasmus shouted "All we were told was to find some young elf in a kingdom where *there are no elves*! For all I knew we were chasing down some scarred-up drunk trying to hide from a gambling debt, not some corn-schilling bumpkin who helped her mum and dad milk the cows! You didn't even know you were an elf for the first two decades of your life, why in the hells would you assume that *I* knew, or even cared who you were until we wound up as forced roommates?!" Erasmus could see Enna was still scowling at him, but with less fire in her eyes, and the quivering lip of someone who had probably never dealt with even half of the things she had in the last week. Erasmus closed his eyes and let out a heavy sigh, trying to regain his composure. "Enna, I was never planning on turning you over to the person who paid O'doc and me, not after I realized that you were our target. You've not done anything to deserve whatever is planned for you."

By this point, Erasmus had let go of O'doc, who had from the onset been more concerned with the burn on his hand than with putting up any kind of struggle. Still, Adrik hovered over the halfling, watching his every move. O'doc looked over to Erasmus. "I didn't want to do that." he muttered. "It's just... I can't risk not finishing a job, not this one..."

"You would allow this to weigh on your conscience for a meager handful of gold?" Adrik shook his head. "For shame, master O'doc! By Othar's beard, what would your family say?"

"This has got nothing to do with my family." O'doc retorted "nor does it have to do with the pay. It's Lannister. He and I have something of a history..."

"What do you mean?" Erasmus asked, raising an eyebrow to his partner. "You and I have been working together for years now, and the few jobs we've done for Ravenclaw and the Rats have been together."

"How do you think I got the head of the largest thieves' guild in the Kingdoms as a contact, Erasmus? He wasn't always *the* Lannister Ravenclaw. When I first left home, I had no idea what I was doing. I was young and clueless. Lannister took me in, showed me the ropes. We made a pretty good team for a couple of years, he and I, but then things started changing. He started making all these power plays among the guilds, something neither of us had ever been affiliated with. I wanted to continue working freelance, doing what I knew, but he wanted to be on top of it all. There was a job he'd got us, just a burglary at a smithy, but it was to be our initiation for the Unseen Hand, the largest guild at the time. Midway through the job there was a snag; the smith was there working late, fell asleep without dousing the forge and a fire broke out. Wouldn't have been an issue if I hadn't dropped some of the goods to try and wake him. The smith ended up getting out safely, but I botched my part of the job, ruined both mine and Lannister's chances at entrance into the Hand. It didn't bother me, but he was furious, said I'd set him back, that I had always been holding him back. He left for Delverbrook that night, and shortly after, I started working with you.

I thought I'd never see Lannister again, until one night he came to me. He and three others snuck into my room as rats, caught me off guard with a knife to the throat. He told me he had a job for me, that I was the best non-Rat he knew, and warned me that if I refused I'd be as easy to find as I was that night. Ever since then, he's been coming to me with jobs, and every time I just hope to all the Gods that it's the last one."

Enna walked over to O'doc, and put her hand on his shoulder. The halfling looked up to see her smiling down at him. "I forgive you." she said, then turning her head to Erasmus "Both of you. I don't know how, but I'm sure we can find some way of dealing with this Ravenclaw person."

"One certainly hopes for as much," Adrik said "however I feel as though this is a conversation for another time and place, notably outside these city walls." He looked to O'doc. "And while I feel your sentiments are genuine, sir, note that if you attempt anything so brazen again, I cannot guarantee that I will show the same restraint as I have presently."

"Don't worry, Adrik," O'doc nodded his head "I'll make a point not to force you to make that choice."

CHAPTER TWENTY-THREE

Varis Liadon awoke groggily to the feeling of a wiry palm striking him across his face as he lay on the floor. "Wake up, you doddering old fool!" shouted an all-too-familiar voice. As the old elf's eyes came into focus, he saw Archmage Derrus Tyn hovering over him, along with a scruffy looking halfling who he did not recognize. "Where are the arcanists that were imprisoned six days ago?" the Archmage demanded.

"Branded and kicked to the streets several days ago, as I had reported." Varis replied groggily.

The elf's answer was met with a boot to the stomach courtesy of the halfling. "Do not lie to me!" Tyn hissed "I've reason to believe you've been harbouring them."

Varis let out a weak, winded laugh. "Did one of your demons tell you that after you bled out a chicken for it?"

Varis felt another boot to his stomach as Tyn leaned down, his face nearly touching the elf's "Listen here, you traitorous piece of filth, I know you've been hiding another one of your kind in these walls, and I mean to find them."

Varis looked up and smiled. "Do you really think me so dense, Tyn, that you think I do not know that you were the one behind the King and Queen's deaths? Or has your bartering with infernal beings simply made you so deluded that you truly believe that everything you have done has been for the good of the Kingdom?"

"I have ensured the unprecedented progress of this Kingdom..." Tyn said, grabbing Varis by his robes "and when all the mortal realm is under Hallowspire's banner I will be heralded as an instigator of peace! I will be recorded in the annals of history as the man who unified the Four Kingdoms against your sly, secretive people!"

"Leave the old elf be." Lannister scowled "He isn't helping us find the one we ought to be looking for." The halfling drew a dagger and began to lean into Varis, grinning maniacally. "If you like, I could slit his throat, keep him from saying anything."

"No." Tyn responded, hoisting Varis to his feet, and holding a dagger of his own to the elf's back. "He comes with us. He's a coward and a survivalist; he will be of use if it means saving his own neck." With a jerk forward, the Archmage began to march Varis out of the chamber, Lannister moving just ahead.

The three spilled out into the hallway, Lannister in front, followed by Varis and then Tyn, his dagger still poking the small of the elf's back. "Alright, elf," Lannister said, looking either direction down the hall "where are you keeping your kin?"

Varis chuckled again, shaking his head. "Are the pair of you really so incompetent that it did not dawn on you the state in which you found me? I was unconscious on the ground, knocked out! Even if I were harbouring an individual, they have clearly made off. How am I to know where they would be headed?"

Lannister turned around, eying Varis suspiciously before turning his gaze to the Archmage. "Your Guards haven't been able to find hide nor hair of Overhill and the dwarf, have they?"

"No..." Tyn said slowly, looking over at Varis and pressing his dagger in. "Where are the halfling and the dwarf?"

Varis winced as he felt the sting of the dagger breaking the flesh. "They are neither elves nor arcanists, they are not your concern."

Tyn twisted some more, causing Varis to let out a small, agonized cry. "Tell me their whereabouts, and I might yet keep you alive to continue withering away as my personal arcane surgeon. Otherwise I'll keep you alive long enough to figure out your trick, and then have you put to death as King Renton demanded all those years ago."

Varis lowered his head and sighed, then raised his head back up, looking to his right. "Down to the first level, in the eastern wing..."

"Very good." Tyn smiled. "We can cut through the throne room, and I can point out to his Grace that I was able to keep you at bay whilst you started to sow the seeds of a fae rebellion." The Archmage shoved Varis forward past Lannister, and the three took off down the hall.

***

It did not take long for the three to make their way to the throne room of Castle Rheth, where King Renton sat holding court, presently granting an audience to a city cobbler. Tyn marched through the stunned, murmuring crowd, Varis ahead of him and Lannister hanging back blending into the crowd the Archmage pushed people to either side as he strode forward until he stood at the foot of the throne, prompting the cobbler to respectfully bow and slink off to the crowd.

"Archmage Tyn!" the King straightened himself, surprised by the sudden interruption "What is the meaning of you barging in here like this?" The King glared at Varis "And what is he doing in my presence?"

"Your Grace, I have come into information that suggests that former Archmage Liadon has been harbouring fae-folk here within the walls of Castle Rheth."

"What?!" the King bellowed, snapping his gaze back to Tyn "How is that possible? What proof do you have of this fact?"

"Nothing concrete as of yet, your Grace. The former Archmage has neither confirmed nor denied the accusations, however I am en route to interrogate two prisoners whom I believe are involved in the plot."

As the Archmage and the King talked, Lannister began to slink stealthily through the crowd. The voices that had haunted him since that fateful meeting had been echoing in his mind since he left Delverbrook, "Bring the elf to Lohvast, by any means necessary." The words rang louder now in his mind as he snuck in his practiced way behind and to the left of the throne, remaining hidden in the shadow of a nearby pillar. Silently drawing a large, ornate dagger hidden beneath his cloak, the halfling whispered, in a voice that was only partially his own "By any means necessary..." before leaping out of the shadows toward and unsuspecting King Renton Isevahr.

CHAPTER TWENTY-FOUR

Enna, Erasmus, O'doc and Adrik moved hastily through the winding halls of Castle Rheth. Erasmus led the way, hoping that he would be able to remember the route Varis had taken them when he had taken them from their cells six days prior. Erasmus had donned Adrik's ratty tricorn hat, as with each new turn he and Enna would need to scout the approaching corridor for any King's Guards on the lookout for the dwarf and O'doc, and he was without a cloak with which he could conceal his fae ancestry. Avoiding the Guards had not been quite as easy for the group as it had been of Adrik and O'doc alone, as not only were the chambers in which to potentially hide more sparse than the cells in the prisons below, but there was also the disadvantage of the fact that the dwarf and the halfling were now likely being actively sought out. The group had been able to traverse the hallways for roughly twenty minutes without incident before turning down one hall that intersected two others, only to be greeted by the sound of heavy footfalls from either direction.

O'doc motioned toward a nearby room, one of three in the hallway, and the only one whose door was ajar. "In here, quick!" he said in a hoarse whisper. The group rushed into the small room as quickly and quietly as possible, with O'doc gently closing the door behind them. The small room was windowless and had no lit candles, and as such Adrik was the only one able to make out any of the surroundings. "Hopefully they'll just pass by." O'doc thought aloud, only to have his hopes for such shattered as the footfalls reached the outside hall, and were accompanied by the sound of the opening of the doors for the rooms at either side of the one the group occupied.

"Damn it all..." Erasmus said under his breath.

"Hold, friends." Adrik said quietly "I've a plan." he corralled Enna, Erasmus, and O'doc up, leading them to the corner of the room alongside where the door was hinged to the wall. "Now be still, and do not fret." he said, before moving quickly to the opposite side of the door, where he drew his mace, and waited.

Both pairs of footsteps reached the door, and with a low creak it slowly opened. There was a flash of brightness as the door opened, made doubly luminous by the fact that one of the Guards was carrying a small lantern. Enna, O'doc, and Erasmus remained in their corner, still shrouded by the shadow of the now opened door, while Adrik remained poised in his own corner. "Right then," the guard not holding the lantern cried out "if you're in here, come out nice and slow." The guard holding the lantern slowly started to swing it in the direction of Enna, O'doc, and Erasmus. Adrik was about to leap out at the pair, but he abruptly held on account of what unfolded first.

As the guards walked far enough into the room to be clear of the door, Adrik watched as Erasmus quickly slammed the door behind them. Before either guard could react, the half-elf wrapped his hand around the trailing Guard's face, pulling his head back and slamming it into the sturdy wooden door. O'doc darted in behind the lantern bearer, slicing the back of his calf, and causing him to cry out and drop the lantern. The halfling then passed around the front of the injured Guard quick as a flash, and with his free hand unclasped his cloak, draping it over the broken lantern to snuff out the flame, then took the Guard's head with both hands and drove it into the stone floor, the helmet making a resounding clang as it hit.

Adrik simply stood in the darkness for a moment, taking in the scene that lay before his eyes. With a chuckle, and shaking his head, the dwarf walked over to the door and opened it up, illuminating the room enough for Enna to see two King's Guards lying unconscious on the floor as Erasmus cracked his knuckles and O'doc shook the broken glass from his cloak, tearing off a strip and bandaging the Guard he had injured.

"By Othar's beard, I gather you gentlemen have done that dance before."

"Let's just say it's not the first time we've been chased into a dark room by people who were after us." Erasmus shrugged "We were lucky this time, too, more often than not we're chased in; we had the element of surprise this time around."

"Do you always bandage up the ones you slice open?" Enna asked, looking at O'doc.

"Not usually." O'doc answered matter-of-factly. "This man was just doing his job. Most of the time my and Erasmus' pursuers are men who've done far worse than us, and would probably take great joy in wringing our necks. In those cases, I'll go for the back of the knee."

"Have you ever needed to go for their neck?" Enna asked.

O'doc and Erasmus looked to one another, neither saying anything. "We're going to have to find an easier way to get through this place." O'doc said finally "After this mess is found, they'll be after us in force."

Adrik looked at the Guards, then looked back up, first at Erasmus, then at Enna. "This suggestion may seem along the far side of ludicrous, however at this juncture I gather anything might be an improvement from our current state of conspicuousness. If all of you would be so good as to assist me in relieving these men of their vestments; I'm of a mind that we should find them far more advantageous than they would at the moment."

The group went to work, using one of Erasmus' short swords to bar the door, and salvaging the candle from the broken lantern for illumination. In no time, they had removed the outer armour from both guards, leaving them in only their chain mail hoods and shirts. While Adrik and O'doc dragged the guards to the corner where everyone but the dwarf had previously been hiding, Enna and Erasmus were trying their best to put the armour on. Enna was having the greater difficulty of the two, as her slight frame was not especially conducive to the bulky plates that made up the armour. With Erasmus' help, she pulled the leather straps as tight as possible on each piece, which was incredibly uncomfortable, but at least made the armour look halfway passable on her.

"Are you sure this will work, Adrik?" Enna asked as she placed a helmet snug on her head.

"It will certainly be far less conspicuous if two fully armoured guards, incongruous of height, were to be seen escorting a pair of ruffian escapees out in plain sight than to have guards come across four suspicious looking individuals slinking about the halls as if all of them had something to hide."

Enna nodded in agreement, and the four exited the room, walking down the halls two abreast, Erasmus holding Adrik in front of him, and Enna doing the same with O'doc. It took little time before the four came across another Guard wandering the halls, her back turned to them. Before the Guard could spot the group, Erasmus made the first move. "You there!" he called out, causing the Guard to spin on her heels and walk toward them. Once the Guard approached them, Erasmus spoke slightly softer, but still in a much more stern voice than his usually casual timbre. "We found the escapees. Should you see any others tell them there is no need to continue looking, and should you or anyone else come across the Archmage, inform him of the arrest."

The Guard gave the pair a salute, then turned her attention to Enna, looking her up and down surreptitiously. Enna, sensing the Guard's eyes on her, spoke up. "I know, I look ridiculous." she said. "Can you believe the smith was supposed to have my armour ready for me three days ago? Instead I've been stuck wearing whatever's left over in the barracks..."

The Guard shook her head, and through her helmet, Enna could see a smirk forming. "Typical old Rikk," she said with a soft chuckle, "Probably got lost in some ale after he got the order and hasn't remembered since; wouldn't be the first time he's done that to a new recruit. Tell you what, I'll swing by his smithy tonight and give him what for. Meantime, next time you need some armour that's a bit more... form-fitting, come look for me, I've got a spare suit that actually has room for breasts in the breastplate, as well as fabric for binding." She held out her hand to Enna. "Name's Brey."

"Tessa, and this is Merrick." Enna shook the Guard's hand, smiling genuinely, in spite of the situation. "And thank you."

"Not a problem." Brey replied. "You both just let me know if you need anything at all."

"Actually," Enna said "We got ourselves a little turned around hunting down these scoundrels. Would you be so good as to point us in the direction of the prisons? Merrick here is so nervous about looking professional that he hasn't dared ask anyone for directions."

"Men..." Brey shook her head at Erasmus before pointing out behind her. "It isn't far from here, just continue down this hallway until it ends, then right, and then if you want to you can take a shortcut through the Throne Room. Just be sure to keep a low profile through there because court's in session right now. From there, it's the next two lefts, and the entrance down is the large, plain-looking oak door with two guards keeping watch."

"Fantastic." Enna smiled "Thank you so much, Brey." Both she and Erasmus shook hands with the guard once more before heading off in the direction she had described.

"Milady, may I say that I am most astounded by your diplomatic abilities." Adrik whispered when they were far enough away.

"Well, I may just be a bumpkin," she said, trying to look sidelong at Erasmus "but I've learned a thing or two about dealing with people in all my years helping my father schill corn and milk cows."

The group continued toward the throne room, finding a noticeable absence of Guards after their interaction with Brey. "This is far quieter than it ought to be." O'doc observed. "There's no way word could have spread that quickly about our apparent recapture."

It was as the group rounded their first corner and approached the entrance to the throne room that they began to hear the dim murmur of a panicked crowd. Quickening their pace toward the direction of the noise, they came upon its source, as well as the reason for the sparseness of Guards; the entrances on either side of the room were barricaded by four King's Guards apiece, ensuring no one got in or out. Erasmus approached one of the guards. "What's going on?" he asked.

"The King is being held at knife point by some halfling screaming bloody murder about an elf." The guard replied "Everyone at court flew into a panic, and we're not to let anybody pass."

O'doc's eyes went wide. "Lannister..." he whispered "Guard! I think I know that halfling, and I know what he wants. Please, let me pass through!"

The guard looked down at O'doc with incredulity. "Who does this one think he is?" the guard asked Enna "He must be hard of hearing, because I just said no one gets in or out of the throne room, least of all a halfling that looks like he's on his way down to a prison cell!"

"You don't understand," O'doc pleaded, looking back at Enna "I know who you're dealing with, I can help!"

Enna looked at O'doc, unsure of what to say. On the one hand, if this was the Lannister Ravenclaw of whom the halfling had spoken earlier, then he would indeed know the mysterious assailant better than anyone, and that could be a great benefit. On the other hand, however, how could she know that O'doc wouldn't seize the opportunity to turn her over to this Lannister Ravenclaw, for his own sake? She looked to Erasmus, whose gaze went from O'doc to meet hers. The half-elf gave Enna a slow nod, and turned his face back to the guard.

"The halfling here is a sell sword known throughout the Four Kingdoms." Erasmus told the guard. "His reputation has him associating with all manner of street vermin, all the way up to the heads of notorious thieves' guilds. It is entirely possible that he is telling the truth."

"And why should I have reason to let so unsavoury a character past?" the guard retorted "Why should we trust him?"

"As you can see," Enna responded "the halfling is under arrest. We will continue to hold him in cuffs and supervise him." She shot the guard a stern look. "Our King's life is at risk right now, if something were to happen, would you really want it to get back to Archmage Tyn that you refused to let pass what might be the only potential help in this castle?"

The guard stared back at Enna a moment, then to Erasmus, before stepping to the side. "If that halfling causes more trouble than what's already taking place, it's on your heads."

"Duly noted." Erasmus said as he and the others rushed into the panicked throne room. "When this is over, I'll offer the Archmage my commendation for your cooperation."

The four had little trouble fighting through the crowds, as most of the people who had been at court were now trying to scramble for the doors. Enna and Erasmus had let go of O'doc and Adrik, duly because of the fact that it helped all four to manoeuvre through the crowd, and because there were no guards paying any attention to them presently. Some from the crowd stayed relatively close to the event unfolding, primarily either out of fear or sheer morbid curiosity. Looking through the few layers of onlookers, the four were able to see King Renton standing upright at his throne, the knife at his neck being held by a halfling that Erasmus and O'doc recognized to be Ravenclaw. They were also able to see at the base of the stairs leading up to the throne a robed elf whom all four assumed to be Varis, also being held at knife point by a wiry man in flowing ornate robes of his own.

"Right then," Lannister cried out into the crowd "Perhaps I wasn't being perfectly clear before: I know there is an elf hiding somewhere in Hallowspire, and unless someone tells me something quick, this Kingdom's going to be without a King!"

"Are you insane?!" Tyn cried out to the halfling "These people will know nothing! This was not part of the Mission!"

"The Mission's changed, Archmage!" Lannister snapped back "And I'd not be surprised if your predecessor there knew a thing or two about who we're looking for..." The halfling turned his head left and right to the members of the King's Guard flanking him several feet back, pressing his blade closer to the King's neck. "And don't you lot think of getting a step closer, or you'll have his blood on your heads!"

King Renton, in spite of the blade at his throat, glared at the Archmage. "Mission? Elf? Derrus, who in the Hells is this thug, and what is he talking about?!"

"I will explain once all this has passed, your Grace." Tyn responded, trying his best to appear calm and in control.

Through the crowd, Lannister heard a familiar, rough-hewn voice call out his name. Much of the crowd in front parted, and what appeared to be a member of the King's Guard stepped forward, a dwarf and another, smaller guard at either side. The guard removed his helmet to reveal the familiar face to whom the voice belonged, that of Erasmus Stonehand.

"Ahh, Erasmus, so good of you to join me." Lannister sneered "As you can see, I've had to come and finish yours and the lamb's job, so I'll be needing that down-payment back once I'm through here."

Erasmus casually took a few steps forward, all eyes upon him. "Funny you say that, Lannister. First of all, I'm not sure that I recall attempted regicide as being part of the job, but then, maybe you and I just have different methods. Secondly, I found your elf." The half-elf

~ 114 ~

gestured theatrically back to Enna, giving her the subtlest wink. "She is yours for the taking."

Lannister's eyes narrowed, focusing in on Enna. "Well then, let's see them."

Erasmus gave Adrik a look, tipping him off to the fact that there was some underlying plan amid the half-elf's actions, and started to play along. The dwarf walked over to Enna and mocked forcing her to kneel, and then proceeded to remove her helmet.

Lannister's eyes moved slowly back to meet Erasmus'. "Just what are you trying to play at, bard?"

"What do you mean? You paid me three hundred gold crowns, Hallowspire gold if my memory serves me, as well as an agreed upon seven hundred at completion, to sneak into this Kingdom, find an elf relatively twenty years of age, and deliver either him or her to you. Well, here you are!"

"Do you think I'm really that stupid?!" Lannister spat. "I can bloody well see that this girl's a human! What was you plan, find the cheapest whore at the first brothel you found and try to pass her off on me? You and your idiot partner would have been better off trying to give me a damned shaven dwarf!" The halfling looked about the area. "And where is the lamb, anyway?"

It was at that point that Lannister, his senses honed from all his years as a thief, felt movement behind him. The halfling instinctively pulled his dagger from the throat of the King just in time for it to meet the blades of O'doc Overhill's daggers.

Archmage Tyn turned his head to the girl kneeling not twenty feet from where he stood. Was that half-elf telling the truth? Could the girl be the elf that had been such a thorn in his side? "Do not move." the Archmage said coldly as he threw Varis to the ground and strode toward the girl. If this was the elf, then he would no doubt be heralded and rewarded handsomely for her dispatch. If not, he reasoned, then it was but one innocent life sacrificed in the name of the Mission; he was sure It would not oppose his reasoning. The Archmage's focus was so squarely upon the girl that he almost did not notice the half-elf charging forward to protect her. Reaching up and clasping his amulet with his free hand, the Archmage opened his mouth to being an incantation with which to dispose of the pesky interloper, he felt his right leg explode in pain as Adrik Thornmallet's mace flew from where the dwarf was standing, shattering Tyn's kneecap and causing him to fall to the ground in agony.

The Archmage looked up at the dwarf, his eyes filled with a white hot rage. "You foolish cretin!" he howled "You shall suffer for having interfered with the Mission!" The Archmage reached out his hand, and spoke in a language that was neither common, nor Elvish. Rather, a deep, throaty bellow that sounded as if it was the voice of not one, but many, came forth:

"UOINOTA IXEN!"

As Tyn spoke the words, his eyes rolled back, taking on a glowing red hue, and from his outstretched hand burst forth a brilliant gout of flames, their colours not orange and yellow, but wholly unnatural shades of red and black. Adrik stood paralysed by the sight, the eldritch crackle of the flames drowning out any other noise. The dwarf shut his eyes, expecting the dark jet to engulf him upon impact. Instead, he felt intense heat surround him from every direction but could feel no flames, as though something was causing the fire to dissipate before hitting him. In an instant, Adrik opened his eyes to see that the flames had ended, and Varis Liadon standing in front of him, smoke emanating from the elf's body as he collapsed on the marble floor.

The sight of the infernal fireball forced the entire throne room into a moment of complete silence. Upon completion of the spell, Tyn went limp, his eyes returned to their usual ice blue. Adrik, Erasmus, and Enna rushed over to the smouldering form of Varis, who upon inspection was still breathing, though the breaths were shallow, laboured, and evidently painful for the elf.

O'doc and Lannister stood, both distracted from their duel by the sight. "What power..." Lannister whispered before hearing a familiar voice in his mind.

"All is lost at Castle Rheth." the voice spoke. "Take flight; go to Lohvast."

The halfling took the opportunity of the pause to try and take one final jab at O'doc's throat with his dagger. O'doc parried the thrust just in time, causing Lannister's dagger to jerk upward, slicing O'doc along his left cheek. O'doc cried out, dropping one of his daggers as he put his hand to his face, and looking as Lannister, rather than trying for another charge fell to one knee, grimacing in pain as he grasped his left shoulder.

"To Lohvast, now!" the voice commanded the halfling. "Serve the Mission and you will be afforded the ability to exact retribution tenfold."

"Yes, I shall." Lannister spoke under his breath, before looking up to O'doc and flashing him a yellowed, sickly grin. "We're far from finished, Lambkins. Best keep one eye open at all times." Lannister slunk down the stairs and took off into the crowd. O'doc grabbed the dagger he had dropped, and was about to sprint after his adversary when he felt a broad hand on his shoulder. The halfling spun around to see King Renton standing over top him.

"Guards, after the one who assaulted me!" the King bellowed "And two of you take Archmage Tyn to a prison cell; He will be tried for conspiracy to commit treason!"

"With respect, your Grace," O'doc sighed "Ravenclaw will be gone before your Guard can even start to find his scent."

"We will see." The King said looking down at the halfling. "In the meantime, we must attend to Archmage Liadon, and further, while I thank you for saving my life, I have many, many questions for you and your friends."

"Fair enough, your Grace," O'doc said, turning to look at the mess at their feet "I'm just not sure how you'll feel about all of the answers."

CHAPTER TWENTY-FIVE

Derrus Tyn lay on a rigid cot in a musty prison cell below Castle Rheth. His broken leg throbbed, and his head echoed the rhythm. In spite of his present state, however, the disgraced Archmage was not fearful or desperate. Rather, as Tyn lay on his rigid cot, he allowed a peaceful calm to wash over him. Though he knew he was in trouble, he also knew that It would come to his aid. He had served It well in the years since he first swore his oath to It, been faithful in following the instructions It imparted unto him. He never questioned the reasoning behind Its wanting Hallowspire to become as it had, free from fae influence, nor did he ever question the means by which It instructed him to achieve Its goals. He knew only that everything he did for It was part of something greater; part of the Mission, and that his assistance in it would be rewarded tenfold with powers unimaginable. Indeed, Derrus Tyn was certain that his faithful work would not go unnoticed, and that now, in his time of need, It would come to his aid, so that he may continue his service. Tyn felt himself smiling confidently through his pain, about to allow himself to give in to his exhaustion, when he heard It speak.

The unmistakable voice of many speaking as one resonated in Tyn's mind, amplifying the pounding sensation in his head. "Derrus Tyn!" The voice bellowed his name so loudly in his mind that Tyn clutched his temples in a futile effort to dull the noise.

"Yes!" Tyn answered back. "I am here! Your humble servant requesting your aid in a moment of need."

"You have failed the Mission." The voice spoke in a unified monotone.

"What do you mean?" Tyn asked, all of the sudden feeling his confidence evaporate. "I have served the Mission, to the letter of your wishes, for the past thirty years!"

"The level of your influence on the affairs of Hallowspire was an overestimation." the voice responded flatly. "As such, three decades of effort have proven to be in vain."

Tyn's mind began to race. "But, there is so much more that I can do to help!" he pleaded "I know that my present situation may cause you to question your faith in me, but this was but a single misstep, a minor snag that can be easily remedied. Please, grant me a boon to aid me in my time of need, and..."

"Silence!" the voice resounded, causing Tyn to fall from his cot, clutching the sides of his head in an agony so great that he did not even notice the pain of his broken leg as he fell. "You were granted a boon for your service when first your pact was agreed upon! You were afforded powers far greater than any mortal you had ever known, powers with which you could have served at Our right hand. Instead, Derrus Tyn, they were powers wasted; squandered away by a mortal unfit to wield them. No, Derrus Tyn, you shall be granted no further boon from Us; your usefulness to the Mission has withered, and as such your service is no longer required."

Tyn tried to speak, to plead with It, but was unable to say a word. He felt a heat begin to form in the pit of his stomach, a sharp burning sensation that began to grow, both in reach and intensity, becoming unbearably hot at its core as it reached Tyn's extremities. As if by some act of merciless punishment, Tyn remained completely awake and aware as the heat reached its peak from within his body, beginning to escape by way of dark flames licking up on his flesh. The flames engulfed Tyn as he writhed, unable to scream, until finally, after what seemed like an eternity, darkness overcame him, as both he and the flames that coated him extinguished.

It was several hours before a guard came across what remained of Derrus Tyn, former Archmage of Hallowspire. The guard, passing by as part of his regular watch, caught the faintest, pungent stench of burnt flesh emanating from the cell, and approached it to investigate the source of the odour. Looking inside, the guard felt a deep wave of nausea sweep over him, causing him to cover his mouth in an attempt to quell the urge to vomit at the sight; what was left of the former Archmage Derrus Tyn lay on the floor of the cell, a twisted, blackened husk, still smouldering. The entire sight was so unbelievably ghastly that the guard could not help but stare, and yet the part of it all to which his eyes were unable to avert their gaze was the centre of the corpse's chest, wherein a strange symbol, almost a kind of brand or sigil, glowed dimly, showing no sign of fading.

CHAPTER TWENTY-SIX

In a simple bed, in a chamber not far from the throne room of Castle Rheth, Varis Liadon lay dying. How the old elf survived the infernal flames in which he had been bathed, he had not the slightest idea, but as he lay there, Varis was acutely aware of the extent and severity of the injuries he had sustained from Derrus Tyn's attack, and knew that it would not be long before he would succumb to them.

The elf had the opportunity to speak with King Renton, his King, and mend bridges that both parties had no doubt thought irreparable. Varis spoke with King Renton at length, insomuch as his weakened, fading state would allow, about the true nature of the now disgraced Tyn, and of the state of Hallowspire after decades of manipulation at his hands. The King begged the elf's forgiveness, a sentiment that Varis took to heart, but declined on the basis that he himself was far from innocent, and that Renton's requests for penance would be wasted on him. The two spoke a few moments longer, before being joined by Erasmus, Enna, O'doc and Adrik. Following the attack in the throne room, the four were given access to whomever and whatever they needed within the castle walls, and at the polite behest of King Renton were cleaned up and tended to. All had bathed, and been given a fresh set of clothes, save for Adrik's tricorn hat, with which he vehemently refused to part ways. The cut along O'doc's cheek had been stitched, and would no doubt scar, and yet the halfling did not seem overly concerned with it. As the four entered the chamber, they approached the foot of the bed in which Varis lay, somber smiles on their faces, belying their obvious melancholic states.

"Varis..." Erasmus was the first to speak after a brief period of silence "you look well..."

The old elf let out a weak laugh, as little could be further from the truth: every inch of Varis' skin was blistered and red, he could barely open his swollen eyes, and the bandages that covered much of his body, his third redressing, were stained with various fluids. "I am dying, Erasmus. The apothecary did what he could, an admirable job at that, but I was struck by infernal fire, the kind of sorcerous conjuration that cannot easily be healed. As it is, I thank the Gods that I have this little time left, to speak with you all, and to set you on your way."

"What do you mean?" Enna asked.

"Derrus Tyn's display today was a step toward confirming what I had long been fearing; the denizens of the Infernal Realm may be at work, and I believe that their aims are ultimately the conquest of the mortal realm." Varis coughed weakly before continuing. "I believe that everything that has happened in Hallowspire in the last thirty years has been a part of a grander plan, being forged by powers far beyond what you or I have ever seen."

"How could you have suspected all of this and done nothing?" O'doc asked.

"I was blinded by spite and pride..." Varis slowly shook his head. "I felt betrayed, and so I lived the life of a coward, biding my time, confident that if the mortal races fell, that it would be punishment for their greed and arrogance."

"Then it was my fault." the King interjected "I betrayed you, and in doing so stole away your trust and respect."

"You were a bereft child, swayed by the venomous words of an opportunistic snake." Varis retorted "There is no blame to be had in your actions." He began to cough hard, stricken with unbearable pain with any breath deeper than a shallow wheeze, and turned his attention back to the four at the foot of the bed. "I digress. You all have seen the destruction wrought by one who swears fealty to demons. I allowed myself to become indifferent to the idea of such destruction in the name of self-preservation, and may well have aided its progress as a result. This is my penance, and yet I fear it has done little to assuage what is to come." The elf closed his eyes, his breathing increasingly shallow, and spoke barely above a whisper. "Forgive me for my part in what is to come, and prepare yourselves, for there will be death." The room was silent then, save for the faint wheezing that was the final breaths of Varis Liadon, until that, too, ceased, leaving behind a noiseless void.

Tears were shed, human, elf, dwarven, and halfling alike. Rites were spoken to different Gods in different tongues, and the mournful group left the chamber, saying nothing, allowing several servants to enter the chamber so as to tend to the elf's remains. King Renton silently escorted them all to a small, humble bedchamber, its walls lined with bookshelves full of musty books and scrolls. "Before Archmage Liadon summoned you, he made it his final wish that all his arcane tomes be left to the four of you." The King looked at Enna and Erasmus "He spoke of the two of you as his protégées, saying he saw in you both a wealth of potential."

Erasmus nodded slowly and forced a smile. "That was kind of Varis to say, your Grace, but I'm a bard and a mercenary."

"And I am far from even beginning to understand arcana." Enna added.

"Well, be that as it may," the King continued "Archmage Li... Varis... insisted on passing his possessions on to you." The King looked over the solemn group. "Further, there is the matter of how I should thank you for your bravery in coming to my aid today. Land, titles, gold, you all need but say a word, and it shall be done. It is a small price to pay for my gratitude."

For a while, no one said a word. As it stood, Adrik had said nothing since the incident in the throne room. Finally, O'doc spoke up. "Your offers are incredibly generous, your Majesty, but the fact of the matter is that none of what any of us did today was out of the hopes of remuneration. I think I can speak for all of us when I say that all we'd really need is Adrik's cart that was seized on market day, and maybe a couple hundred coins between the four of us so that we can get Enna home to her mum and dad, and get the rest of us heading our own ways."

King Renton pursed his lips through his beard and nodded. "I'll see to it that it is done, and that I have you off and on your way before sundown, and I'll send you off with one thousand crowns each and hear no arguments on the matter." The King's eyes passed over each one of the group. "Further, know that you are, each and every one of you, and your kin as well, honoured guests in my Kingdom and my Castle. I have made many a decision in my time on Hallowspire's throne, many of which I now find myself bringing into question. You are all instrumental in that, and for that as well, you have my thanks." The four all gave low, reverent bows, and King Renton Isevahr replied in kind.

The arrangements were made, and as promised, Adrik had his cart and mules returned to him, and with the sun hanging low and red in the sky, the dwarf's cart loaded up with the tomes left to them, the four departed from the city of Rheth. Erasmus and O'doc sat in the back of the cart, Erasmus playfully chastising his partner about the arrangements.

"He was willing to offer each of us a thousand crowns!" the half elf jingled a large purse in O'doc's face. "You should have asked him for two!"

"Well I didn't hear you piping in." O'doc responded with a smirk.

"Ah, well." Erasmus shrugged "Go figure that: we didn't even finish the job we were hired for, and we still wound up with more than what Ravenclaw offered us!" He slapped the halfling on the back playfully. "I think we managed to do alright."

O'doc let out a slight chuckle, and looked out to the road. He ran his hand along the stitching were Lannister Ravenclaw had cut him across the cheek, a cut that would scar over, and serve as a reminder, not only of how lucky O'doc was for Lannister missing his throat, but also of the fact that Lannister Ravenclaw was, indeed, still out there, very much alive, and no doubt very much looking for revenge.

Enna sat up front next to Adrik, giving him directions for the route back to her home. The dwarf remained silent, saying nothing even when the group was giving their goodbyes to the King. Instead, Adrik Thornmallet sat in silence, guiding his mules when Enna told him where they needed to go, and looking as though his gaze was out further than just the road ahead, but stretching as far as the peaks of the coastal mountains of Lohvast.

They rode like this for some time, until finally, Enna turned to the dwarf, his eyes still as dead ahead as they had been for the past three hours. "What happened to Varis, what he did, it wasn't your fault." Enna noticed the slightest hint of Adrik's violet eyes looking sidelong at her, before returning his gaze to the road. Enna sighed, and looked down, noticing the pendant hanging from her neck. She held it up in her hand

and began to examine it. "You know," she said "I think this pendant you gave me is my arcane implement."

"I do not have the slightest guess as to why that may be the case, Milady." Adrik quietly responded, keeping his eyes forward. "I have no means or knowledge in regards to enchanting objects, that was simply a piece that I was selling years ago at Rheth's market day that happened to catch the attention of a young girl and her mother."

"Maybe it's nothing special to you, Adrik," Enna replied, still looking at the pendant "but it meant the world to me, and it still does, even more so now. Maybe an implement doesn't need to be enchanted to work, maybe it just needs to have a connection to whoever is using it."

"That would certainly explain me and Caster." Erasmus piped up from the back, stroking his mandolin lovingly. The half-elf gently adjusted two of the tuning keys, before strumming a soft melody, and serenading his companions with an old tune that he found particularly fitting:

Bright summer sun turns to pale winter moonlight,
Another dawn shall these old eyes never see,
But mourn me not, child, though I go from your sight,
For ever in your heart shall always I be.

Do not fear the world, though 'tis wild and vast,
I know you'll be oh so much stronger than me,
And though your journey begins as mine has passed,
Forever in your heart shall always I be.

So hold close your kin and your dearest of friends,
To join you both in sorrow and revelry,
Hold them close as I have held you until the end,
For in their hearts, as yours, shall always I be.

So look now with me to my final sunset,
Then go forth to adventure, untamed and free,
As I breathe my last breath, I've no worry, no fret,
As forever in your heart shall I always be.

The group was quiet for the remainder of the journey, the kind of comfortable, contemplative quiet that Enna had become used to with her father. Adrik was thankful that the sun had finally set, as by the light of the moon, none of his companions would be able to see the tears that had begun to stream down from his violet eyes. Enna had been right, what happened in Castle Rheth was a matter of circumstance, the kind of which the dwarf had seen all too often in his life to that point. The friendships he had grown with the three individuals surrounding him, however, were the kind that Adrik had not seen or felt for so long, the notion had almost been forgotten to him. It was for that, the gratitude Adrik felt swelling within him, that he silently wept.

Chapter Twenty-Seven

Nighttime hit the rural trade roads outside Rheth quickly, bringing a bitter autumnal chill with it, and as much as Enna longed to be back home, and the others longed to be as far from Rheth as possible, all decided that there was no sense pushing themselves any more than they had already, and that one night camping on the road was not too great a diversion from their initial plans. O'doc, who had managed to fall asleep in the back of Adrik's wagon earlier in the trip, took first watch as the others slumbered. He thought back to the previous day, the duel with Lannister, and the look in the other halfling's eyes when Derrus Tyn conjured that black fire that had been intended for Adrik, but ended up taking the life of Varis.

O'doc compared Lannister's eyes with those of everyone else he could think of in that throne room. Most were frightened, horrified, or at the very least shocked. Not Lannister Ravenclaw, though, whose bright yellow eyes had a very distinct look within them. The look was something O'doc had seen numerous times when the two were partners, most notably when the pair would case a particularly wealthy merchant or noble to pickpocket, or a well-appointed manor to burgle. It was the look that Lannister had when they had first met with the middling members of the Unseen Hand at their opulent guildhall. It was a look of greedy longing, as much as it was one of sizing up a challenge.

When Lannister Ravenclaw got that look in his eye, it meant that he saw something or someone that was richer, or more influential, or more powerful than he was. Further, the look meant that Lannister would do everything in his power to obtain whatever caused it, no matter what the cost.

All of the sudden, O'doc heard what sounded like the snap of a twig near where the four had made camp. Grasping his daggers, he sprang up, silent as a cat, and began to cautiously step toward the area. Another twig snapped, and the halfling looked over to the direction of the noise, the small dirt patch where the group had earlier set a campfire. The area was still dimly lit, as the last embers glowed, and O'doc, straining his eyes, was able to see a shadow moving about. As he approached the campfire, he noticed that the shadowy figure appeared to be rummaging about the goods left there. O'doc quietly snuck up, until he was almost upon the apparent thief, crouched low, and leaped forward to strike, only to have his blades deflected as the figure swung around and raised a club defensively. O'doc reacted quickly, tumbling back and spinning around to see a shocked Enna Summerlark standing before him.

"Enna!" The halfling said in a hoarse whisper "Why are you awake? And what in Shendré's name are you doing?"

"Never mind that," Enna shot back in a similar whisper "why did you just try to attack me?"

"I'm on watch!" he had to try not to yell.

Enna looked at the ground, embarrassed. She didn't want to admit that she still had misgivings about O'doc because of what had happened in Castle Rheth, in spite of the fact that he had not shown even the slightest sign of malice toward her since. "I'm sorry," she said, still looking down. "You're right. I just haven't been able to sleep, and you startled me..."

O'doc sighed and shook his head, placing his daggers back in their sheaths at his hip. "Well, you're up now, may as well start your watch shift." Enna nodded, and the two walked back to where O'doc had been keeping watch before. Enna sat against a tree, and the halfling sat next to her.

"You aren't going to get some sleep?" she asked.

"I'm still wide awake." he shrugged "especially now that your rummaging got me all uppity."

"Sorry again..." Enna replied. She looked at the club, turning it over in one hand, and running the other against its gnarled shape, ending at the top, which had a large piece of amber seemingly embedded into it. "I wanted to find this."

O'doc looked over at her. "One of Erasmus' swords would

probably make you feel safer during your watch." he said.

"It's not for that." she replied, reaching one hand up to hold her pendant "I wanted to find some way to, I don't know, put these together or something." She looked over at the halfling "I must sound like I've gone mad." she half-laughed.

"Hardly." he said, holding out his hands to take the club from her to examine it. "A pendant is hardly an ideal arcane implement. It forces you to lower your defences when you reach for it, it serves little practical purpose in close combat, and it could easily be torn from your neck, or worse, used to strangle you." O'doc stood up, holding the club as one might hold a rapier, and took a fencing stance. "Now some manner of wand or short staff, such as this, can be far more multifunctional." He began to move about, thrusting and parrying at the shadows. "If caught in close quarters, it can make for an effective improvised weapon." The halfling then changed his stance, narrowing it, grabbing the club closer to its top, and holding his free hand outward. "And, of course, from afar, it allows you to cast while still maintaining a readied position." O'doc eased himself down, walking back to Enna and handing the club back to her. "I think it's a fine choice for a naturally gifted arcanist."

"Thank you." Enna smiled back at him. "It looks like you've used your fair share of weapons, and you certainly know quite a bit about arcana for a..." she stopped herself.

"Thief? Sell sword? Smuggler?" O'doc smirked "...killer?"

"I'm sorry..." Enna blushed "I didn't mean to..."

"It's alright," O'doc raised a hand to stop her "I've heard worse, and yes, I have lived something of a *sordid* life, but I was raised well."

"Really?" Enna tried not to sound too surprised.

"Is it so hard to believe? After all, you're an elf who spent her whole life raised by human farmers, and who had everyone convinced she was human as well. Looks can be deceiving." Enna didn't respond, leaving O'doc feeling embarrassed. "Look, I didn't mean..." he thought for a moment. "It seems like you get along well with your parents."

"You don't?" she asked.

O'doc looked into the blackness of the night. "There's a reason why I do what I do." he said "I don't suppose you've heard of the Overhills of Kahlen Ridge?"

Enna shook her head.

"The halfling owl-riders of Ghest?"

Again, she shook her head.

O'doc raised his eyebrows in amazement, looking back to Enna. "Renton really did keep you lot in the dark, didn't he?" He looked outward once more as he continued. "The Overhills, my family, are a long, proud line of halflings that hail from northern Ghest, in the great woods of Khalen Ridge. Bigger trees than you'll see anywhere in the Four Kingdoms, and owls to match. My father, Odo, swore service and sword to the goddess Shendré, like his father before him, and met my mother Ornella when he was charged with defending the Arcane University of East Fellowdale from a group of orc marauders from Majadrin. She was studying there, one of their brightest students. They were married as soon as they were able, and he retired from the adventurer's life, choosing instead to open a martial academy in Khalen Ridge, while she continued her own personal arcane studies.

"I was the third child of four, and the only one who showed no interest in either my father's love of the sword or my mother's love of arcana, and little natural talent in either field. Sixteen years of being the odd one out can wear on a person, I suppose, and it got to the point where I just needed to find my own way in the world. That was over a decade ago..."

"Have you ever been back home?"

The halfling shook his head slowly. "I was too young and stubborn when I left, and then after I got involved with Lannister, well let's just say that the less he knew about me, the better it was, and the safer they were."

"Well, what about now?"

O'doc opened his mouth to speak, but closed it, unsure of what to say. "I suppose..." he stammered "I don't know what I'd say to them now... or what they'd say to me..."

Enna placed her hand on the halfling's shoulder. "If your parents are anything like mine, your dad will give you a hug so tight you'll likely struggle to breathe, and your mum will tell you to make sure you scrub your hands clean before you even think about laying them on the fresh rye loaf she just spent the whole day on." O'doc smiled a melancholy smile, and looked over at Enna, who had a tear rolling down her cheek.

"I miss them," she said "I know it's only been a week, and we're just a few hours away, and they aren't even my birth parents, but I miss them so much."

O'doc placed his hand on hers. "Never mind," he said "Adrik and I shared a prison cell with your father our first day in Rheth, and the whole time there were two things he talked about, your mother, and you. You're more than just what you were when you came into this world. As my father often used to say 'a bard makes more coin singing of acts than of titles', and as far as I can tell, you act as much like a daughter to your parents as they act like parents to you."

Enna sniffled and nodded, a smile reappearing on her face. "Your dad sounds like a very wise person."

O'doc nodded. "He always was quick with advice." he paused, and looked down. "I'm truly sorry for my actions in the castle."

"You were afraid," Enna replied. "We all were."

The two sat together in silence for a very long while, the only sounds to be heard were the crackling of embers and the whistle of the autumn wind. "I do miss those owls." O'doc said, feeling himself start to doze off.

"I'd like to see them someday." Enna yawned.

After dawn had broken, Adrik and Erasmus awoke, and looking around the campsite, found Enna and O'doc, laying with their backs against a large tree, sleeping peacefully next to one another.

CHAPTER TWENTY-EIGHT

In a small tavern called the Bastion's Tap, Kavis Hindergrass, a middle-aged man wearing a plain shirt and apron, polished a tin stein, one of roughly one hundred and fifty, as a fire crackled softly in the hearth opposite the simple oaken bar. The barkeep looked about the empty tavern floor, which had been slow enough to close early for the first time since market day, and let out a heavy, relieved sigh. It seemed that for the past week patronage had expanded tenfold, likely due to the tavern's proximity to Castle Rheth.

Typically, a handful of the King's Guard would stroll in throughout the day to have a pint come the end of their shift, but the recent deluge of customers were largely varied. Some were farmers, some were merchants, some were shop keeps, and some were even other barkeeps. One thing they all were, however, was nosey. Word had spread round quickly enough on market day about a rogue arcanist that was arrested in the streets. Not an uncommon rumour, but not typically one that had much staying power. Still, as the week passed, the rumours began to broaden: there was word that the arcanist was a fae-folk, and that the traitor Varis Liadon had been spotted with them.

Yesterday had been the most outlandish, however, with talk that there was not one, but two fae-folk, as well as a halfling assassin, and a dwarf, all who were apparently at court where Archmage Tyn summoned flames black as night from his hands. Kavis shook his head as he recounted the tall tales, usually started by the guards themselves, likely in hopes of getting a free drink or two out of it. The barkeep's thoughts were interrupted by the sound of his cat, who was making a low growling noise by the corner nearest the entrance to the tavern's kitchen.

"What're you on about then, Hunter?" He asked, placing the stein on a drying rack and walking toward the cat. "Find a little beast, have you?" Kavis approached the corner to see through the door what his cat was growling about: on the other side of the threshold was a large grey rat with black eyes, standing on its hind quarters. The rat was larger than any Kavis had ever seen, and seemed, beyond the barkeep's reasoning, to be scowling at the now hissing cat. "Oi, get you gone you nasty vermin!" Kavis shouted as he turned around and grabbed a nearby broom with which to swipe at the rat. As he turned back however, Kavis stood stunned, his cat hissing and backing away as the rat began to grow in size, its features changing. The rat's hair began to thin and recede as it grew, and its features seeming to soften in a way, giving it a more humanoid form. In a matter of minutes, the rat that had been scowling at Kavis' cat was a male halfling, standing naked in the doorway which led from the tavern floor to the kitchen.

The halfling looked down at himself and made a face, as though his nakedness was more inconvenient than embarrassing. He looked back up to the barkeep. "I swear, you've got to have a fresh pair of clothes around every corner if you want to be able to be an effective lycanthrope. I could use some pants, if you've got a spare set nearby." Kavis Hindergrass did not move or speak, but instead fainted from sheer disbelief of what he had just witnessed. "Well then," Lannister Ravenclaw said, turning to the barkeep's cat and flashing a crooked grin "looks like I've got the run of the place."

Lannister looked through the tavern, finding some clothing that he was able to cut down to a manageable size, a cudgel behind the bar, likely the barkeep's for emergencies, and a sparse amount of coin, also likely the barkeep's for a different kind of emergency. Looking around the back of the tavern, the halfling was able to find a small stable and, unable to find any ponies readily available, opted for a smaller mule over a full-sized horse. While he was not especially pleased with his ramshackle supplies, Lannister was at something of an impasse. He was forced to change into a rat for his own survival after the debacle at the castle, and as such was forced to leave behind all his supplies. Further, he had a limited window of time left in which Rheth's main gate was still open for the day, and had no desire to spend yet another day on the streets avoiding cats, dogs, and people who did not watch where they were going. And so, Lannister Ravenclaw hopped up onto the mule, goading it to the main gate of Rheth as quickly as it would carry him, and left the city, thankfully, he noted, without incident.

The halfling rode on for days, unsure of where he was headed exactly, knowing only that he had been commanded to go to Lohvast, and trusting that whatever was waiting for him in the Kingdom of the Clouds would be trying to find him.

Lannister's journey was slow going. The mule was not a particularly speedy mount, doubly so because the halfling was riding bareback. Further, most of the journey took place at night, so as to assuage any suspicion that any other travellers might have regarding a halfling in oversized clothes riding a mule bareback. Lannister's night time travel helped as well, inasmuch as it was far easier to procure goods for the road from sleeping caravans than it was from awake and alert ones. All in all, it was nearly over a week's travel before the halfling began to see Lohvastine flags being flown. By this point in his journey, Lannister had passed enough poorly guarded travellers that he was wearing clothing that fit: a pair of cotton shirts and two pair of pants, as well as a leather vest and boots that, while they were roughly a size too small, were still far nicer than having to travel barefoot. It was at this point in his journey, as well, that Lannister began to once again hear the voices.

Unlike his previous incidents, when the voices spoke to Lannister now, they were more dulcet, more relaxed. "You have done well in serving the Mission," they would say, their tone still relatively unified, but not as harsh and commanding as it had been prior. "Go to Frostpoint, the village at the northwestern base of the Celestine Mountains. Show your allegiance to the Mission, to Us, and you shall be offered power unequivocal."

"I shall." Lannister answered, spurring the mule in the direction that the voices directed. "Give me strength, and I am Yours, Your servant in the Mission." The halfling's answer, his willingness to agree to servitude, was not characteristic of him, and yet the voices' promise of power, and of revenge, seemed to cause Lannister to want to give himself over to the Voices' commands willingly.

It was another three days of travel, but finally Lannister arrived, exhausted and road worn, in the small town of Frostpoint. The town was, in actuality, more of a hamlet, serving as a way point between the Lohvastine capital city of Heavenguard and the Great Arcane University, the last remaining in the Four Kingdoms. Lannister was unsure as to what to do now that he had arrived in Frostpoint, as the voices had been silent for the last two days, but he was sure of two things: he needed a room, and thanks to the frigid winds that blew down from the Celestine Mountains, he needed something heavier and warmer than a couple of cotton shirts and a leather vest. Thankfully for the halfling, his various evening campsite ransacks had yielded him a fair amount of coin as well, and upon discovering an inn called the Moon and Shine, he tied up the mule to a nearby hitch and sauntered inside.

To call the Moon and Shine a dilapidated shack would be a disservice to dilapidated shacks. A tall burly man stood behind an old bar that was visibly uneven, splintered, and covered in stains that Lannister, possibly due to the poor lighting of the establishment, could not determine the origins of. For that matter, the lighting was so bad that Lannister was unable even to determine the barkeep's origin, as someone of that size could just as easily be an average sized half-orc as a particularly large human. The sparse tables were largely empty, save for a lone hooded figure sitting at the far side of the tavern floor, at a table nearest the stairs. The halfling shrugged indifferently at the surroundings; he had stayed in far worse accommodations in his life, and in all truth nearly any bed would be a step up from the last ten days of sleeping on the ground. He strode up to the barkeep, sitting on a tall stool so as not to have to strain his neck looking up any more than necessary at the tall man's, or possibly half-orc's face. "I'd like a room." he said "And if there's anywhere in town where I could get a cloak, I'd appreciate that information as well."

"The rooms are twenty-five crowns a night." the barkeep grumbled, his back turned to Lannister as he cleaned the spigots of the kegs behind the bar. His voice was gruff, and had an accent that allowed Lannister to pinpoint that he was, in fact, a half-orc.

"Twenty-five crowns a night?!" the halfling cried out. "Have you been sampling your wares all night? That's more than I've paid for overnight stays at lords' castles!"

"Then go find a lord with a castle." the barkeep shot back. "Otherwise, twenty-five crowns a night."

"I refuse to pay."

"That's fine." the barkeep turned around and looked down at Lannister with a hard face, his stone grey eyes matching his skin. "If you like, you can sleep out in the cold with the horses, or maybe you could head back to Heavenguard, that's only about a day's travel on horseback." the barkeep scratched the stubble on his chin in mock contemplation. "Oh! If you were an arcanist at the University, you could stay there, but then why would you be asking me for a room, and too stupid to come to Frostpoint without a cloak?"

Lannister stared up at the barkeep, his anger welling up, when he heard the sound of a hand slapping what sounded like a coin onto the bar. He looked over to see the cloaked individual from the back of the tavern sliding whatever they had placed down across to the barkeep with a slender hand. "This halfling means no trouble, Ohr." the voice, a female's, said. "He is with me, and his room and board have been taken care of."

The barkeep picked up the piece, which appeared to be some manner of large coin or medallion, and upon inspecting it, hurriedly pushed it back to its owner. "Of course." He said, his gruff voice now tinged with anxiety. "You have the key already, help yourself."

"Thank you, Ohr." The cloaked woman nodded slowly, then turning herself to Lannister, who was unable to see her face under the cloak in the dark tavern. "Come with me, Guildmaster," she said. Lannister followed the woman as she turned and began to walk toward the back of the tavern, past where she had been sitting, past the empty kegs and barrels, to a plain wooden door. As she opened it, Lannister looked into it and saw only unlit blackness. The cloaked woman stood aside, holding the door open, and gesturing for the halfling to enter. Lannister tentatively obliged the woman, and after taking a few steps in, only going as far as the scant outside light was able to illuminate, he heard the door begin to shut behind him, and before he could even turn around, Lannister was plunged into pitch blackness.

"Hello? Anyone there?" he cried out, trying his best to mask the nervousness in his voice. The answer to his question came in the form of a glow, a red and black flame that emerged, silently and suddenly, from the palm of the cloaked woman, who was standing at the closed door. She said nothing, and instead motioned Lannister to move forward, down what now revealed itself as a long stone corridor with a wooden door on the end.

The halfling turned around, genuinely surprised by how well the odd-coloured flame that the woman had conjured was able to light the corridor, and began to walk forward, the glow making it evident that the woman was following behind. The hallway was unremarkable, stone floors and walls, and yet its similarity to the one he had walked in that building back in Delverbrook was such that it gave the halfling a chilling sense of deja vu. Further, Lannister noticed that the corridor seemed to stretch well past where the inn ended on the outside, as if it almost did not exist to the outside world past that simple wooden door at the back of the tavern.

At the far side of the corridor was another plain wooden door with a familiar sigil burnt into it, a sigil the very sight of which caused Lannister's shoulder to ache slightly. His hand shaking ever so subtly, the halfling pulled the door open, revealing an all-too-familiar spiral stone staircase. Every muscle in Lannister's body wanted to turn tail and flee, away from what undoubtedly came next, away from Lohvast, away from the Mission, but he had given his word to the Voices, and his mind, seduced by the promise of immense power, pushed his body forward in spite of itself, down the spiral staircase, to the bottom landing, where a plain wooden door with the same sigil burnt in greeted him, just as it had in Delverbrook.

Lannister pushed the door open, expecting the musty smell of old tomes, and the huge chamber that contained them in floor-to-ceiling bookshelves. He expected hooded men and women of all races, supporters of the Mission, possibly staring at him as he entered, as they had stared at him as he exited. All of this was expected, and revealed itself. What Lannister Ravenclaw did not expect, however, was the raised dais in the centre of the room, with a hooded figure in dark robes standing atop it, holding a bronze goblet in one hand, and a long, curved dagger in the other. The rest of the hooded figures, meanwhile, were in fact staring at Lannister, all the while chanting, a similar liturgical call-

and-response to the one the halfling had heard in his mind all those days ago, the night he left for Rheth.

Almost without having to think, Lannister approached the dais, and bowed low to the hooded figure atop it. "I am ready to give myself fully to the Mission." he said, not knowing entirely where the words were coming from, but having an intrinsic sense that they were the correct ones to say. The figure atop the dais beckoned Lannister forward, and the halfling strode to the top of the stop of the dais. Much like the woman in the tavern above, Lannister was unable to see the face underneath the hood of this figure, and could only discern that it was male when it finally spoke.

"Vi z'ar katima tepohaic confn!" The figure cried.

"Jasi nishka faestir Udoka algbo!" the rest responded in unison.

"Jacida iejir ui hesini!" the figure continued.

"Vur hesi iejir ui jacida!" they responded.

"The arm on which you were branded." the figure said to Lannister, who instinctively stuck his left arm outward. Two individuals from the crowd walked up behind the halfling and rolled up his sleeve, while one approached behind the figure facing the halfling and rolled up the sleeve of his robe, revealing an arm covered in strange, eldritch tattoos. Each of the followers then held each respective sleeve up, while the third held Lannister by his shoulders. The halfling then watched as the figure in front of him gave the goblet to his assistant, who then held it underneath. Then, pressing his forearm up against Lannister's, the figure took the long, curved dagger, and cut a large slit across both. Lannister flinched, unable to hold back a cry of pain as he felt his blood run down his arm, mixing with the blood of the hooded figure, and dripping into the goblet being held below. After several minutes of this, two of the assistants wrapped linen around each of the wounds, and all stepped away, the one holding the goblet passing it back to the hooded figure, who then held it up to Lannister. "Drink." he said. "Drink, and you shall be forever bonded to Us; you will know His name, you will gain His power, and you will serve His Mission, Our Mission."

Lannister took the goblet from the hooded figure, and placed it to his quivering lips. The figure, then clasping the base of the goblet, tipped it upward, forcing Lannister to gulp. The cup's contents were hot, hotter than boiling water. The heat surged down the halfling's throat, reaching his belly, and exploding outward, igniting every fibre of his being. Lannister felt his mind explode with a fierce, infernal intellect, shared knowledge that was aeons old. In that moment, Lannister Ravenclaw was changed, and raising his head to scream in agony and delight, the voices emerged from him, his now a part of them, and he called out His name, the name of He who set forth the Mission, a name only knowable to those who have taken His power in exchange for their service. Lannister called out that dark, unknowable name, and in an instant fell to one knee, exhausted, panting, and sweating. Two more from the crowd emerged holding a hooded robe similar to their own, approached the dais, and lifted the halfling to his feet, draping the robe over his figure.

The hooded figure on the dais spoke again in the strange tongue, only now Lannister could understand clearly all that was being said. "And so on this night, we ordain a new servant to the Mission."

"May he serve the Mission well." the crowd echoed.

"He shall serve." The figure said "His blood is Ours, and Our blood is his. From this day forth, Lannister Ravenclaw has been granted both burden and privilege; to carry out the Mission, and to smite all who oppose it." There was a final call-and-response, only this time, Lannister Ravenclaw spoke with the others, as one voice.

"So has it been said,"
"So has it been heard,"
"So has it been understood,"
"So shall it be done."

CHAPTER TWENTY-NINE

Tessa and Randis Summerlark sat anxiously in their kitchen. One week ago, Randis had come home with a pair of King's Guards, and without his daughter. One of the guards, a man not much younger than Randis, handed him a note upon his release. He and Tessa read it immediately after the guards had left, and it read as such:

Master and Lady Summerlark,
This note shall be the first of what I imagine will be many, as for the time being, I have taken charge of your daughter. Know that, though I have my own reasons for holding her in my care, that these reasons are not dubious, and that in my taking this action I am, in fact, keeping her far more safe than she would be otherwise. For this reason, I implore you not to make any effort to contact your daughter, nor to make any attempt to return to Rheth and retrieve her, as any such actions could compromise the delicate nature of her safety. I am well aware of who and what your daughter is, and I stress again that I will not lay my hands upon a single strand of her hair, and that you can feel secure in knowing, daily, that I am protecting her from those forces that would. I shall remain in touch.
Regards,
Varis Liadon

Randis held Tessa in his arms as she cried, as much from fear as from anger and confusion. Varis Liadon, the former Archmage? Rumours said that he had died decades ago. Even if he was alive, why was he doing this?

Over the next several days, a member of the King's Guard would come near sunset, the same older man who had delivered the first note. The notes that followed were shorter than the first, often stating simply "You need not worry. Enna, and her secret, are still safe." Always, the notes were signed by Varis Liadon. On the third day of this, Tessa, who always met the guard to receive the notes, asked the man "Is the former Archmage alive?"

The guard nodded "Yes, milady, though most outside the Castle think it otherwise."

"Why is he doing this?"

"I do not know the lord's plans, milady." he answered "I am simply instructed by him to ride to your farm daily and deliver a note."

"Do the King or the present Archmage know about any of this?" The guard was silent, and Tessa looked at him. "Why are you so willing to help a known traitor?"

Without having to stop and think, the guard responded. "Milady, I am not a young man. I have served his Grace King Renton as I served his father before him, as that is my responsibility as a member of the King's Guard. When the King and Queen died and Archmage Liadon was tried for treason, I was old and experienced enough to know something was amiss. I was also, however, old and experienced enough to know that I had a duty to fulfil, and a wife of my own who relied on my doing that duty. As such, while I cannot claim any formal allegiance to Archmage Liadon, I am only under obligation to serve his Grace, and not whomever he has chosen as his right hand."

Tessa nodded, and smiled knowingly, something about the guard's sincerity putting her slightly at ease. "Thank you." she said, to which the guard bowed, before turning around to walk back toward his horse.

It had been two days now since that guard had returned, since Tessa and Randis had received any word about their daughter. Both feared the worst, though neither would tell the other what they thought. And so, for the last two days they sat anxiously in their kitchen, waiting for the guard, any guard, a note, anything. For the last two days, the Summerlarks sat in their kitchen, silently waiting for a glimmer of hope, though it now began to feel as though they were really waiting for the hope they had to run out.

Both Randis and Tessa perked up at the sound of something approaching their home. "Do you hear that?" Tessa asked, turning to her husband.

"I do..." Randis replied, a look of caution on his face. "That's too great a noise to be a single person on horseback, though. It sounds more like a wagon." Randis stood up and walked over to the back door of the house, picking up a hatchet that was propped up against the wall. "You stay where you are, Tess." he said as he crept toward the house's main entrance. "If anyone's come looking for trouble, I'm in just the mood to oblige them." Reaching the front door, Randis stood to one side of it, back against the wall, and slowly pulled it open enough that he could see through the small crack who was approaching. Tessa, poking her head through the threshold between the kitchen and the front entrance, saw her husband drop his hatchet to the floor, his face going as white as linen. "By the Gods..." he said, before swinging the door open and running out, prompting Tessa to chase after him.

Reaching the open door, Tessa looked in amazement as she saw Randis running toward a wagon being pulled by two mules, and driven by a dwarf that looked quite familiar. Two of the passengers she did not recognize, but the one sitting next to the dwarf, the reason Randis ran out of the door in a flash, caused tears of joy to well up in Tessa's eyes as she ran to join her husband. Sitting next to the dwarf, and excitedly leaping off of her seat was Enna Summerlark. The family met together in a group hug, tears flowing freely as not a single one of them wished to let go of the other two, as though each feared that doing so would pull them apart once more.

"Mum, Dad," Enna's words were spoken through large, choking sobs. "I've missed you both so much!"

"And we have you, Sweet." Tessa kissed her daughter on the forehead. "We've never been so worried... we're both so glad you're safe."

Enna turned and motioned to her companions, all of whom had dismounted the wagon. "These three are to thank for that: Adrik, Erasmus, and O'doc." The dwarf, half-elf, and halfling all bowed as they were introduced, Adrik and O'doc giving Randis a knowing smile as he stepped toward the three of them.

"You have our thanks a thousand times." Randis looked to each of them as he spoke. "If there is anything in the world, anything whatsoever that we can offer you, please, just say the word."

Erasmus put his hand up to stop Randis. "Please, don't discredit Enna. We all found ourselves in our fair share of difficult situations, and she was just as instrumental in her return here as we are. We really couldn't ask for anything."

"Nonsense!" Tessa interjected, dabbing the last tears from her now red and swollen eyes. "Adrik... Master Thornmallet, if I recall correctly from all those years ago..."

"At your service, now as ever, milady Summerlark." The dwarf bowed once more.

"I take it this is your wagon?" she asked.

"Indeed, as are the mules that serve as its means of travel."

"Well, unhitch those mules. Randis will show you to our stable, where they are free to their share of oats. As for all of you, you are staying the night for a warm meal and a good rest. It is the very least we can do, and I'll hear no words against it."

"Milady, I am confident that I speak for my associates, as well as myself, when I say that we are, all of us, grateful of your hospitality, and would be more than happy to oblige your offer."

"Agreed." O'doc said as he and Erasmus nodded their agreement. "Thank you kindly for the offer."

"Good, it's settled!" Randis said, clapping his hands together before walking to Adrik's wagon. The dwarf followed him, smiling for the first time in days as he drank in the warm atmosphere of the reunion.

Dinner was served late, well past sunset. This was due in part to the hour of the group's arrival and in part to the fact that Tessa not only was cooking for a much larger group than she was used to, but also because she insisted on serving a far more elabourate meal than what she had initially planned. In the meantime, introductions and reintroductions were made, with Adrik more than willingly helping with dinner, and Erasmus providing upbeat, joyous tunes on his mandolin, the whole household coming to life in such a way as the Summerlarks had not seen in years, and had only hours earlier feared that they may never see again. By the time the six had sat down to eat, they spoke as if they had known one another for years.

During the meal, which consisted of roast pig and chicken, stewed potatoes and carrots, and more wine than even Adrik could drink in a single sitting, Enna spoke at length about the experiences she and her new friends had shared in the last week, with her companions happy to interject with any details that she missed. When she arrived at the point in the tale when Varis had revealed to Enna her true heritage, however, she paused. A knot formed in the pit of her stomach, as she was unsure of how to approach what was no doubt a delicate subject.

Randis and Tessa, seeing their daughter's hesitation, looked at one another, and then looked back to her. "Enna, sweet," Randis began, his own stomach now similarly knotted, as he and Tessa had never quite prepared for this moment, regardless of the fact that both knew it would eventually, inevitably arrive. "Your mother and I, well... there's something you should know... about the day you were born..."

Enna smiled softly, taking her father's hand, and looking at both her parents with eyes filled with a mixture of happiness and sorrow. "Mum, Dad... I know what I am... and I know why you did what you did." She reached up and brushed her hair back, removing the cuffs that sat atop her ears, and holding them out in her open hand, looking at them. "I want you to know that I don't blame you, and that no matter what, you'll always be my mum and dad. I know that I'm an elf, but that doesn't mean I'm not a Summerlark."

Randis smiled, and looked back to his wife, who closed her eyes and nodded slowly. Though she was smiling as well, Randis could tell she was blinking away the faintest tears in her eyes. "Come with me," he said, looking back at Enna and standing. "I've got something you should see."

Enna stood up and followed her father out the back door, out past the chopping block and firewood. as they walked, Randis told Enna all about the night when he had found her birth mother, about the elf's last words to he and Tessa, and the couple's decision to hide Enna's elven heritage at all costs. "I want you to understand," he told her "your mother and I wanted to tell you this, all of it, for so long. It hung over us every day, but there was just no way we could take that chance, not with the way things are here."

"I understand, Dad," Enna replied. "But I think everything that happened at Castle Rheth really had an effect on King Renton. I think things might be changing in Hallowspire."

"Hopefully for the better." Randis said, half to himself. Not far from the chopping block and firewood, in a thick patch of wood at the very edge of the Summerlark property, Randis stopped walking, Enna stopping next to him. He knelt down, and pointed toward a small patch of ground where a bush of chrysanthemums wilted and browned, having been touched by Autumn's chill. "This is the place." he said. "When I buried her, I couldn't well have placed a headstone, for fear it would rouse suspicion, so I planted those mums, because I didn't ever want to forget the spot." He stood up and stood next to Enna, placing a hand on her shoulder. "I can stay with you a moment, if you like."

"It's fine, Dad," Enna replied, her eyes transfixed on the dying flowers. "I'll be alright."

Randis nodded, giving his daughter a kiss on the forehead. "Take all the time you need, sweet. We'll all be waiting for you back in the house." He wrapped his arms around Enna, giving her one more strong hug before turning and heading back inside.

Enna stood there for a moment, simply taking in the scene around her. The leaves in all the trees had gilded or browned, and the light breeze in the air caused many of them to gently dance to the ground around her. She closed her eyes, and allowed it to wash over her, the same feeling of familiarity she had all those times when she would sit and meditate, except now she had finally begun to understand the feeling. Perhaps there was something left behind, some kind of connection to the fae realm that this elf, Enna's birth mother, had brought with her all those years ago. Enna opened her eyes, and sat, cross-legged, on the cold dry ground. The only noise she could hear was the sound of dry leaves crackling beneath her. She sat in silence for a moment, simply looking at the chrysanthemums. "I... am not really sure what to say..." she said at last. "I mean, I never knew you, I don't know that I'll ever even know your name, and yet I wouldn't exist without you." She sighed deeply. "I should be angry, furious even about all of this... but instead... it's just as if I have this whole big part of myself that isn't there, like a book that you didn't know was missing a chapter, or a song that you just found out has a new verse, except no one knows how that verse goes. I can't be angry because I don't know enough about you to be *anything*, and that lack of something... well... it needs substance. I need it to have substance." Enna got up, and turned to leave the makeshift grave. After a few steps, she turned around, "One more thing. I don't know who you are, or how or why you ended up where you did when you did, but I turned out alright as a result, great even. I thought you might want to know that, seeing as you're my mother and all..." she paused, allowing the weight of what she said to sink in. "I hope I would have made you proud." Enna turned back toward the small cottage on the Summerlark homestead, and started on her walk back home.

When Enna walked back into her house, she was greeted by her parents and her friends, all sitting at the kitchen table, seemingly waiting for her to return. She smiled, in spite of how heavyhearted she felt about what she had to say. "I did some thinking out there, while I was talking to my... um... elf mum, I guess..." she looked to Tessa, who she was relieved to see did not seem upset by that. "I was only gone from home a week, and I missed it so much, but while I was gone I found out that there was this whole part of who I am that I never knew about. Ever since then my mind has been filled with questions, and I know that there are only so many that you can answer." Enna looked down, as though doing so would soften the blow of what she was about to say next. "I can't go on leaving those questions unanswered. I don't know how, but I need to find answers, closure. I want you to know, though, that no matter who, or what I find, you'll never stop being my family." She looked up, she was not crying; there had been enough tears shed that day, and she would not let any more fall. To her surprise, however, everyone else seemed to be smiling.

"Enna," her mother said "Your father and I knew that when the time came you'd no doubt want to go out and find your heritage."

"We got to talking, all of us." Randis looked down the table at O'doc, Erasmus, and Adrik. "Your mother and I, we can't go with you, much as we'd like to; there's the farm to run, the Gods know I'm not the spry young merchant I once was, and truly what young lady wants her parents tagging along as she goes to see the world?" Enna let out a laugh, feeling slightly better upon seeing her father's grin through his salt-and-pepper beard. "Now it seems to Mum and I that these gentlemen have earned your trust, something we taught you to be wary of giving out too easily. Not to mention, they're the lot of them far more worldly than you."

"Dad..." Enna said in an admonishing tone "did you ask Erasmus, O'doc, and Adrik to put their lives on hold for my sake?"

"Hardly!" Randis answered "We offered to pay them to be your guides."

"Dad! You can't just..."

"Relax, Enna." Erasmus interrupted. "We didn't take any payment."

"Indeed." Adrik added "The decision was a unanimous one, and the idea of receiving remuneration in order to aid a friend in her journey of self-discovery? Well, milady, I shudder at the very notion!"

"Besides," O'doc smirked "we're still sitting on all that gold King Renton gave us, we can afford a little time off work."

Enna opened her mouth to protest, but could not. Instead she simply smiled, indescribably grateful for those in the room. "Thank you, all of you." she said.

"Well, it's decided." Tessa sat up. "Where will you go?"

Enna thought a moment, then shook her head. "I'm not really sure where to start..."

"Well, if you're looking for information on elves, then someone who knows a thing or two about arcana would be a good place to start," O'doc reasoned. "Luckily for you, I happen to know someone in East Fellowdale."

"That sounds wonderful." Enna replied.

"Sensational!" Adrik cried out, clapping his hands together. "To Ghest! We depart tomorrow morning!" He looked over to Enna and bowed apologetically, realizing that he got caught up in his own excitement "...provided that the arrangement suits milady."

"It's perfectly fine, Adrik." Enna smiled. With a plan put into place, the group said its good-nights, all promising to rise early enough for the companions to be on the road before midday.

Night came and went, and everyone under the Summerlark roof found that they had, for the first in too many nights, slept restfully. All awoke to the sound of the rooster's crow, and began making preparations for the journey. O'doc and Adrik drew out routes on one of Randis' old maps from his merchant days, bickering over routes more than they agreed on them. Erasmus helped Randis dig up as many supplies as the pair could find, namely warm cloaks and furs, as well as all manner of equipment for cooking, camping, and an old longbow with a handful of arrows "because you can never be too careful," Randis reasoned. Enna and Tessa gathered cured meats and preserved vegetables for the road, Tessa insisting that Enna and her companions were in much greater need of them than she and Randis. Everything was packed up in Adrik's cart, and as O'doc and Erasmus hitched the dwarf's mules up, last goodbyes were said.

Adrik rummaged through the back of his cart, and emerged holding a number of ornately carved green stones, all polished to a resplendent sheen. "Now, I am well aware that Sir and Milady will refuse any reimbursement for last night's hospitality," he said, walking toward Randis and Tessa "however it seems that there is scant room for travelling supplies in my cart, and I feel there is no other reasonable course of action than to leave this Braashine malachite with the two of you." He smiled and winked at Tessa. "I do hope that it is not a burden on Milady to have to find space for these pieces."

Tessa let loose a small laugh. "No trouble at all, Adrik, I'm sure I can find somewhere to stash them away."

"Excelsior! Well, fare thee well, Summerlarks." Adrik bowed low. "Howsoever we are able to contact you with tales of our exploits, I will oblige you most assuredly."

"Farewell, Adrik Thonrmallet," Tessa said as she and her husband bowed in return before turning to their daughter. Tessa hugged Enna tight. "Be safe," she said, fighting back her inevitable tears. "And good luck. We hope you find what you need to find, and please, remember that this is always home."

"Of course, Mum," Enna squeezed back "and thank you, both of you, for everything."

Randis pulled his daughter in for a hug so tight it nearly drew the breath from her. "Be good, sweet," he said. As he released his hug, he reached into the folds of his shirt. "I have something for you, before you leave."

"Dad, it's alright." Enna said "between the four of us, we've got more than enough money to get by."

"It's not money." Randis smiled. "You're as stubborn as your mum, so I knew not to try and win that fight." He pulled something out, holding it in a closed fist. "It's not much, but Adrik helped me make sure they looked good enough to wear on such a pretty face." Randis opened his hand to reveal a pair of gold ear cuffs, similar to the silver ones Enna had worn for so many years, except for one major difference in design: the cuffs Randis held in his hand extended out at the back tip, coming to a point, so as to resemble the ears of an elf. "It was the least I could do, seeing as I took them points off your ears in the first place..."

Enna looked at them, stunned, as tears filled her eyes. "Oh, Dad..." she wrapped her arms around Randis once more "They're beautiful, perfect. Thank you."

As Enna let go of her father, he wiped her tears from her face, though more flowed in their place, then brushed her hair back, removing the silver cuffs and replacing them with the gold. Randis, now, began to fight back tears. "Prettiest elf I've ever seen." He smiled "I always told you how much I love when you wear those."

Enna shared one final embrace with her parents before climbing onto the front of the wagon. "I'll be back," she said as she climbed, "I promise!"

With a crack of the reigns, the mules began to amble down the dirt path away from the Summerlark homestead. "It would appear," Adrik said "that contrary to what we had all foreseen initially, our escapades together are but in their infancy! Onward to Ghest, and as such, to East Fellowdale..."

Before the dwarf could finish, his companions shouted out in unison "What ho!"

EPILOGUE

In the grand throne room of The Great Spire of Heavenguard, Merrian Arkalis, Queen of Lohvast sat, smiling contemplatively. Occasionally the Queen would come to the large chamber, high up in the castle's fortress-like structure, and bask in the sun's rays as they beat in through the stained glass windows that surrounded most of the chamber. The Queen was smiling because she had just heard news from Hallowspire; The Archmage Derrus Tyn was dead. Another nail in the Great Bastion of Humanity's coffin.

Queen Arkalis did not need any convincing of the fact that Lohvast, her Kingdom, was the greatest of the Four: Majadrin was a far-flung desert wasteland run by orcs, barbarous humans, and the spawn that result from their unnatural commingling. Ghest, while it was indeed prosperous, had so little unity that it could scarce be called a Kingdom, as King Meklan Van Hyden was too fat and lazy to deal with his subjects, preferring instead that they take care of themselves nominally. And then there was Hallowspire, the Great Bastion of Humanity. The very title made the Queen chuckle every time she heard it. Lohvast's closest neighbours had so much potential, but it was all squandered away on a shell of a King and a megalomaniac Archmage who would have done anything in a desperate bid for power. She would know; she attended the Arcane University in Lohvast with Derrus Tyn.

Lohvast, on the other hand, prospered. Under Queen Arkalis' careful watch, trade, arcana, and loyalty all flourished. If Hallowspire was the Bastion of Humanity, then Lohvast was the Crown of the World. It only made sense, the Queen thought to herself, that the rest of the world ought to be taught to agree.

"...Your Grace?" The quiet, almost fearful voice of Archmage

Tavon Elbar pulled the Queen from her thoughts.

The Queen looked over to the short, scrawny man in the gold and purple robes of her Kingdom, a bemused look playing across her porcelain face. "Are you still here, Archmage Elbar?"

"Yes, your Grace." Elbar bowed apologetically. "You have not yet responded to the news."

"Well you clearly did not relay it loudly enough for me to have taken notice." The Queen retorted testily. "Now repeat it, and by the Gods, try to have your voice escape your lungs this time!"

"Of course, your Grace." Elbar bowed yet again. "News comes from Hallowspire that Archmage Derrus Tyn is dead. As such, King Renton is requesting that we send three or four of the most apt arcanists from the University to Rheth so that they might be canvassed as candidates for the Kingdom's new Archmage."

Queen Merrian tapped a long fingernail to her chin, thinking for a moment. "Very well," she said finally. "Archmage Elbar, you are to assemble five hundred of the finest Warmages the University has to offer. Appoint a leader among them, someone naturally commanding, and bring them to Heavenguard for training."

Elbar's eyes widened, taken aback by the order. "Is... that all, your Grace?"

"One final thing," the Queen looked at Elbar, a sinister grin playing across her face. "Whomever you appoint to lead the Warmages, have them deliver a message to King Renton: Lohvast is formally declaring war."

About the Author

Brandon Draga was born in 1986, just outside Toronto, Ontario. His love of all things fantasy began at an early age with games like *The Legend of Zelda*, *Heroquest*, and *Dungeons and Dragons*. This affinity for the arcane and archaic led to his studying history in university from 2005 to 2011. In late 2012, he began writing a D&D campaign setting that would lay the groundwork for the world of the Four Kingdoms. Brandon still lives just outside Toronto, and when he is not writing enjoys skateboarding, playing guitar, and playing tabletop games.

More Titles by Realmwalker Publishing Group

The Riven Wyrde Saga by Graham Austin-King
Book 1: *Fae: The Wild Hunt*
Book 2: *Fae: The Realm of Twilight*
Book 3: *Fae: The Sins of the Wyrde* (Fall 2015)

The Echoes of Imara Series by Claire Frank
Book 1: *To Whatever End*
Book 2: *An Altered Fate*

The Rotting Frontier Series by Dave Atwell
Book 1: *Rotting Frontier*
Book 2: *Rotting Frontier: Revelations*

The Young Gods Saga by J. Daniel Batt
Book 1: *The Young Gods: A Door Into Darkness*

Keaghan in The Tales of Dreamside **by J. Daniel Batt** (Fall 2015)

The Realmwalker Chronicles by Lee Aarons
The Pillars of Natura, Volume 1: Maior
The Pillars of Natura, Volume 2: Halen
The Pillars of Natura, Volume 3: D'Ware (2015)
The Pillars of Natura, Volume 4: Nym (2015)

The Flowerday Papers by Stephanie L. Mitchell
Book 1: *Illumination*

**Find us at Amazon, Barnes and Noble, and other fine
bookstores everywhere.
To order from us direct:
www.realmwalkerpublishing.com/order**

CPSIA information can be obtained at www.ICGtesting.com
Printed in the USA
LVOW06s2256240815

451348LV00002B/4/P